whisper of memory

Whispering Woods #2

Brinda Berry

Copyright Warning

Published By Sweet Biscuit Publishing LLC
Cover Design by Najla Qamber Designs

Whisper of Memory
All Rights Are Reserved. Copyright 2012 by Brinda Berry

First electronic publication: March 2012 by Etopia Press
Second electronic publication: October 2014 by Sweet Biscuit Publishing LLC

Digital ISBN: 978-0-9916320-7-7

Print ISBN: 978-0692316412

About the Author

Brinda Berry lives in the South with her family and two spunky cairn terriers. She's terribly fond of chocolate, coffee, and books that take her away from reality. She doesn't mind being called a geek or "crazy dog lady." When she's not working the day job or writing a novel, she's guilty of surfing the internet for no good reason.

Social media at:

http://www.brindaberry.com
https://www.facebook.com/BrindaBerryAuthor
https://twitter.com/#!/Brinda_Berry

For release news, subscribe at

http://www.brindaberry.com/mailing-list.html

Acknowledgements

Special thank you to Thalia S. Child. This would not have been possible without great editing, guidance, and dedication.

Dedication

This is dedicated to my first readers for this book, Audrey and Maddie; my technical advisor, Jake; and my inspiring niece, Lindsey.

Chapter One

Portal

The dead leaves formed an ocher carpet on the ground that spoke in crunchy whispers as I backed up two steps. Watching the leaves begin to whirl like a waterspout in the ocean, I waited. I identified the spot before I heard the buzzing or saw the air lifting the leaves. Even before I saw the sienna-orange veil drape over the ground, the tingly sensation moving through me from head to toe told me it was a portal.

I smiled in anticipation of seeing Regulus today. I wanted to spend every afternoon and weekends together, but he had college classes, and I had high school. Next year would be different. We'd attend Whispering Woods U together.

Daydreaming about my boyfriend could be a dangerous mistake.

The glint of the metallic blade almost blinded me before I ducked to avoid losing my head. Most dimensional travelers carried something quite a bit smaller. More portable. The Amazon-sized woman standing in front of me carried the samurai sword like it was a Gucci purse. But I respected the blade and the woman. I never underestimate the danger of any situation. Last week, a traveler, otherwise known as a Slip, had beaned me using a weapon similar to a slingshot. It hadn't mattered that he'd looked like a seven-year-old boy. The Slip had aimed the weapon with deadly accuracy and left me with a bruise the size of a baseball.

Now I said, "You should back up and return to your home, lair, crib...whatever you call it. You are unauthorized to travel to this area." I thought my voice sounded firm, yet pleasant, like an airline stewardess telling an unruly passenger to return to her seat.

The woman's eyes widened, and she tilted her head. She stopped circling me and planted her feet in a fighter's stance. She looked to my left and right and smiled, as though realizing I was alone.

A whistling sound was followed by her surprised expression before she fell to the ground on her knees and crumpled in an unconscious heap.

My boyfriend had disabled her temporarily.

"Mia, what do you think you are doing?" Exasperation flowed from his words. Regulus walked around the body on the ground toward me. Arizona strolled two steps behind him with a carefree smile directed my way and lowered the weapon he held. The small silver box looked more like a cell phone than a tool capable of delivering deadly watts of electrical current.

"Just stalling her." I folded my arms across my

chest. "Plus, she caught me standing here. What did you expect me to do? Run and hide until you guys arrived?"

"Yes," they both answered.

Regulus picked up the blade that the woman had dropped when the electrical shock hit her nervous system. Turning it back and forth in his hand, his gaze met mine. Looking down, he poised the blade above his arm and purposely raked the sharp edge across the top of his skin. The light hair on his arm gathered in a line at the end of the blade's path. Regulus blew it to the ground. His dark blue eyes returned to mine.

"Did you know that a decapitated head is still cognizant for up to four seconds after its removal from the body?" He bent to roll the woman onto her back and retrieve the scabbard for the blade.

"Gross." I involuntarily shivered. "I get it. Stop treating me like an idiot. I could feel the buzzing right after she came through, and I knew that you were behind her." I closed the distance between us and lifted the woman's head from the ground.

He tugged the shoulder belt of the scabbard in an effort to remove it. "You can help," he said as he laid the weapon on the ground and held her up by the shoulders. I drew the brown leather straps holding the metal sheath from her body.

He rested his hand on my shoulder, and I lifted my head. His thumb moved to caress my chin. "You are indispensable. How many times must I tell you this?" The words came out low and intimate. He had the furrowed brow that I only saw when he was agitated.

"Lovebirds, we have to get her restrained unless—" Arizona's amused voice was cut short when the woman on the ground grabbed his ankle and yanked him off balance. He hit the ground hard enough to make a wheezing sound as the air punched from his lungs.

Regulus scrambled to seize her arm, but with lightning speed, the woman wrapped both her legs around his waist. She snared his wrist and shoved his head underneath her shoulder. The woman's legs swept up to encircle his neck.

I screamed and tugged at her arms while pulling to loosen the hold. She had drawn her knees forward and tight to her body. I heard Regulus gasp for air and saw him twist, trying to find a way to release himself.

Arizona crouched on his hands and knees looking for something. He swept his hand back and forth underneath the crackling piles of leaves.

"Do something." My frantic voice cut through the woods and stopped him in his search. I realized that he was searching for his weapon.

Arizona picked up the blade that lay atop the fallen leaves. The woman had wielded the weapon with ease, but he held it with both hands. He shook his blond hair out of his eyes and gave me a disarming smile that was totally inappropriate in the circumstances. Circling the two on the ground, he jabbed the end of the blade to her side. "Release him slowly. I wouldn't want to accidentally cut off your arm or disembowel you. You know the sharpness of your blade, and I mean you no mortal harm."

Regulus coughed, and he moved his head out of

her chokehold. He crawled away backward to distance himself while I searched the ground for Arizona's weapon. The shiny box sat inches from Arizona's boot, and I retrieved it to hand to Regulus.

My fingers brushed his, and I looked into his eyes to see anger. The expression made me think he was mad at himself, but I wasn't sure. Without a word, he moved to stand at the other side of the woman and pointed the stunner I had handed him. A sharp sound preceded the blank look on the woman's face. She slumped into unconsciousness.

"Are you OK?" I couldn't stop myself from asking although I knew it was exactly the wrong thing to say. The wind made leaves dance in surreal slow motion across the clearing. I waited for him to turn and answer, but he ignored me. I moved toward him.

Arizona took my wrist to stop me. He shook his head back and forth as he draped the strap of the scabbard over his head. "We have to take the woman to the Vault at headquarters. We'll see you later."

"No, I'll take her," Regulus said. He didn't turn to look at me. "Please make sure Mia gets home safely."

"Regulus, why won't..." I hated whiners and clingers. I trailed off before I could completely embarrass myself. I never cried. Even when my cat Dudley was killed by a coyote and I had to bury her, I hadn't cried. My eyes pricked with the threat of tears, and I turned to walk home.

Arizona followed a couple of steps behind me, saying nothing until we walked a half mile. "He cares a lot for you."

"Yeah, yeah. He shows it well." I shoved my hands into my pockets and shrugged. "He acts like that was my fault. And it wasn't."

"No, he knows. When Regulus isn't perfect, he gets upset. He let his guard down because he's so in lust with you he can't think about his job." Arizona laughed softly. "And don't get mad at me for telling you the truth."

My mouth dropped open. "I can't believe you just said that." I grinned at his mischievous expression. "Yes, you always tell the truth whether I want to hear it or not."

I wondered why I didn't have a crush on Arizona. It would be a much easier relationship. Especially since Regulus was my first boyfriend. And this was my first year of being a gatekeeper for the agency monitoring dimensional travel. My senior year of high school was turning into a real doozy.

"Maybe it is a little my fault." I smiled. "If I wouldn't look all starry-eyed every time I see him, he could concentrate."

"Oh, come on. Now you're trying to make excuses for him. What about me letting her grab my ankle? Whose fault is that? Is that your fault too?"

"No."

"I think it's because the woman couldn't keep her hands off me, obviously." His grin didn't match his serious tone.

"Of course." I answered with the same degree of seriousness.

"If I could only get your friend Emily to see what all the others see."

"Good luck with that."

"I don't need luck. She only needs to open her eyes."

At first Em had talked about how cute she thought both Arizona and Regulus were. The minute Arizona had started paying attention to her, she'd backed away like a scared rabbit.

Arizona slowed his pace. The path through the woods exited onto a dirt road. We walked in the middle of it since no cars were in sight. Whispering Woods, Arkansas had a hundred back roads exactly like this one, deserted and rarely used. Wildflowers that would soon die lined the ditches on both sides.

He cleared his throat. "Does Emily have a boyfriend? She's a very pretty girl. It wouldn't surprise me and would explain her attitude."

"No. Quit trying so hard." I tried to be gentle because I could tell his feelings were hurt. Or maybe it was his ego. "She might come around. I know she thinks you're really cute. And she thinks you're funny." I could tell the last comment made him happy because he smiled. His expression quickly changed as if the light bulb had clicked on.

"Clowns are funny. I'm no clown." His eyebrows lowered.

"Oh no. Clowns are definitely not funny. They're extremely weird and scary."

"Hmm. Maybe I should work on being less funny. She's not taking me seriously."

I switched to a more pressing topic. "Will Regulus take long? I thought I'd get to see him tonight. My dad is home and said he could come over."

Arizona looked behind him and turned back to me. "He'll be along soon. I have orders to get you home."

"And you always follow orders, right?"

"Yes, that's what makes us a good team. Regulus is in charge and that means you should do what he says also."

I saluted him. "Yes, sir. Any more orders, sir?"

"Fix me up with Emily."

I giggled. "You're on your own, buddy."

The log house where my dad and I lived came into view. We stood in silence at the end of the long, winding driveway. I looked over at the wooden shelter that stood at the intersection of the main road and my driveway.

"Wanna sit at the waiting booth and see if Regulus catches up?" I hoped he would agree. My cell vibrated in the pocket of my jeans. I glanced at the cell display before answering. "Hi, Austin."

"Hey, Mia," the deep voice on the other end answered. "Listen, Tiny called me and told me about something. I need to come over. And I'm picking up Em to come with me."

"It's not a good time, Austin." I shifted from foot to foot. "I mean you're always welcome, but Regulus is probably coming over in a little while." I watched Arizona fiddling with the sword that he still held.

"Your brother's in a video online. It's Pete, all right. I'm coming."

I felt the blood rush from my face. Austin had already clicked off.

"What is it, Mia, what's wrong? Are you all right?"

"We have a lead on my missing brother." I ran toward the house.

* * *

"Sweet." The word lingered on Austin's lips while I anxiously watched the video on the computer monitor.

"I don't care about this. Where's the part with Pete?" The video camera was pointed at conference participants walking in the exhibit hall from booth to booth. With five people crowded into the space between my bed and the desk, it was unbearably stuffy. I jockeyed for the best spot directly in front of the monitor. The blinds and curtains were closed to minimize the light in the room. I'd have cleaned if I'd known I would have guests. I wasn't allowed to have Regulus alone upstairs, so he was getting a rare peek at the slob I tried to hide.

"I think it's important to watch the entire thing so we don't miss something important," Em said reasonably. Leave it to Miss Attention-to-Detail to give that word of advice. But she was right.

The video from our recent trip to GameCon had been uploaded by a guy named Tiny, who was the opposite of what his name implied. The hulking giant had become a loyal friend of mine ever since he had pulled off a flash mob at the gaming conference. If it weren't for that distraction, I'm not sure what would have happened.

Em twisted her hair around her finger and nodded at me. "We're gonna find him." She moved a couple of inches away from Arizona who had somehow found a way to stand next to her. He had kicked a pile of my dirty clothes out of the space to be able to stand there. Great.

The music started on the video, and the teens and adults of the flash mob began to swing the fake light sabers at one another in a flurry of choreographed activity. The music filled my head with a deluge of color. It was the hardest and most beautiful part of being a synesthete.

But the best part was being able to locate portals since that talent had brought Regulus into my life.

I concentrated on the screen and blocked my other senses as much as a person can. It's like telling someone to taste the chocolate chip cookie, but don't smell the vanilla and cocoa that makes your mouth water.

"Look, here." Austin pointed to the far right corner of the screen. "See this guy wearing the dark hoodie?"

"Yeah. What's he doing?" I bent closer to the screen. "I can't see his face."

"No, you can't here. But he's going to turn in a minute, and you'll get a full face shot," Austin said. He had moved to sit on the edge of the desk chair and patted it for me to sit with him.

I sat immediately in my eagerness to see better. The players in the flash mob kept time with the music. The figure in the black hooded sweatshirt drifted unobtrusively between the flash mob figures, sliding in and out of the crowd.

The face in the hoodie turned toward the video camera.

"Freeze it." Em leaned forward and squinted. "I don't know."

"It's him," I said.

"Yeah, I'm sure too." Austin never took his eyes off

the screen. "I believed you, Mia, but it's just weird to see him after so long. And he's looking around for something right here. For someone."

"You?" Regulus directed the question at me. He had arrived at my house only minutes after we did. I would never get used to the nonlinear time element of traveling between dimensions. "He told you to be there, correct?" He put his hand on my shoulder, and Austin scooted away slightly in the chair we shared.

"No, I think he's looking around for someone else. Those guys who looked like they bench press a couple of hundred pounds every morning before breakfast," I said.

I clicked the mouse to start the video again. Rapping on my bedroom door caused me to quickly close the video. The door opened. My dog Biscuit gleefully ran into the room at the opportunity. He sailed in one leap onto the bed and ran back and forth in a whirl of happy activity, trying to entice someone to pet him. The golden blur moved between Regulus and Em, as they were his favorite people in the room. My cairn terrier would take petting from anyone, but he seemed to gravitate to certain individuals.

"Hi, Mr. Taylor," said Em. "We're, um, watching videos."

My dad's expression told me that we looked guilty of something, but he didn't know what. "I wanted to tell you that I'm driving into town. I can pick up some snacks if your friends are staying for a while."

"OK." The resounding answers came from everyone but me. I had hoped to spend time alone with Regulus. I could only go out on dates on the weekend, and my Saturday was slipping away.

"Thanks, Dad. You really don't have to do that." My automatic response had a defeated tone, but no one seemed to notice.

"No problem, kids." Dad leaned against the doorframe.

Regulus crossed the room to my dad and held out his hand. "It is nice to see you again, Mr. Taylor. It is always a pleasure to be in your home." He shook my dad's hand.

"Yes, yes. You're welcome anytime," Dad said.

I caught Austin rolling his eyes while looking at the blank computer monitor. He turned back to face the doorway. "Mr. T, you could pick up some movies, and we could all watch them. Together." His huge grin made me want to kick him.

"Oh, I can't stay, and you've got to take me home. I rode with you, remember?" said Emily. She sat on the edge of the bed in a more relaxed position. "We came over to show Mia a killer new music video and visit for a few minutes."

"Don't let me interrupt then." Dad looked at me and then his watch. "I should be back in an hour. Want me to take Biscuit out?"

"No. You can leave him," I said. Biscuit looked very content as Regulus rubbed his head and ears.

"OK then. You kids have fun," Dad said. He shut the door softly behind him.

I opened the Internet browser and brought the video up again. Noticing the stats on the bottom of the video, I breathed a little quicker.

"This video has been viewed over five hundred times since last week. It's going viral, and the wrong person is going to see it. Tell Tiny he has to take it down," I said, getting louder and shriller with each word.

"Calm down, Mia." Regulus's voice cut through my hysteria. "If they were looking for video footage, it would be too late."

"He's right," Austin said in resignation. The fact that he had agreed with something that Regulus said was a small miracle. "Tiny didn't realize that Pete's in the footage. I'm the one who noticed it." Austin cleared his throat. "Tiny did point out something interesting."

"What's that?" I said.

"If Bleeker's people are looking at video footage, then they're looking for Pete. At first, we thought they were only there to find you. Now, I'm not sure. Why would Pete need to be secretive about his whereabouts? It might be good for us to draw their attention." Austin looked from Regulus to Arizona for confirmation. He finally rested his gaze on Regulus. "Either Pete is running from the IIA or from Bleeker's crew."

"He would have no reason to run from the IIA." Regulus's answer was sure and defensive.

Austin eyed Regulus suspiciously. "Why don't we speculate that it's Bleeker's people then? If they know that we are all involved in finding Pete, what would they do next?"

"Force Pete's location from one of us. They might think we know where he is. Which we don't." Em muttered the words to herself.

I started the video again from the beginning and let it play through without stopping to see his face.

We watched Pete move through the crowd and stand at the booth at the end.

"Wait. Go back. What did he do there?" Austin took the mouse away from me to click the controls of the video player. He crowded me on the chair, and I nearly fell off the seat.

"What?" I didn't know what I had missed.

"He signaled someone." Austin sat back and folded his arms in deep thought. "I thought he was alone in this. But he's not. He's got someone...at least one person with him."

"Show us this signal," Regulus demanded.

"Right here." Austin clicked the video back several frames. "Here he rubs his nose and then he holds up one finger." Austin demonstrated the movements in unison with Pete.

Arizona snorted in an unflattering way. "He has an itch and scratched his nose. What does it mean?"

"It's a signal to fake bunt in baseball. What it meant on that day, I don't know," Austin answered. "I've seen it a million times on the baseball field. Can't help it that you girlie men never played baseball."

Arizona shoved Austin, and I fell off the seat onto the floor, my head hitting the hard wood of my desk. "Ow!" I found myself wedged between the bed and desk chair with legs flying everywhere and Em screaming while she pried Arizona and Austin apart. Biscuit barked excitedly and lunged forward to nip Austin.

"That's enough!" Em took Arizona by the arm and led him to the other side of the room. "We don't have time for you guys to act like you're twelve. We have some serious stuff going on."

Em scared even me with her tone. I hadn't seen this side of her. She was usually the silly girl who obsessed over hair and makeup.

The silence in the room was deafening until Biscuit began growling at Austin, who stood with his hands up in the air as though surrendering. We all stared at each other as if seeing someone for the first time.

"She's right," I said. "I know that you guys probably wouldn't be friends if it weren't for me—"

"We're not friends. These dudes are in your life. I can accept that." Austin stared at Regulus. "Bottom line. We all care about you. Or at least I do. They may be using your portal locator sense—"

"Synesthesia." I supplied the word, then continued, "You're going to say something we'll both regret. Stop it."

Em walked to the door with Biscuit wagging his tail as he followed. "Austin, I have to go home. Come on." She smiled, but the emotion didn't reach her eyes. "Mia, I'll text you later. I've been doing more research on the business card that Pete left you, and we can talk when you're alone." She looked at Austin. "Now. Gotta go."

Austin wouldn't meet my eyes.

Arizona watched Em leaving and looked regretful. "'Bye, Emily. I will behave myself next time."

She laughed at that. "No, you won't. But that's what makes you so much fun."

He did a little bow to her, and she winked at him before she turned and went out the door. I questioned if I hadn't just witnessed some bizarre flirting ritual.

"Be careful that Biscuit doesn't get out." I yelled down the stairs after them. He barked when he heard his name. I looked back at Regulus and Arizona. I thought the room would seem less crowded with Austin and Emily gone, but that wasn't the case.

My bed looked like a small tornado had landed where Arizona and Austin had knocked it around while fighting. I straightened the comforter and pillows.

"His hate for me is evident." Regulus sure didn't believe in beating around the bush.

"He doesn't hate you. He got into the fight with Arizona, not you."

"In Austin's mind, Arizona and I are the same. He wished he was hitting me." Regulus rubbed the back of his neck. "And Arizona should not have let his emotions rule him."

"Arizona did shove him," I said. "Austin talks trash, but he doesn't mean anything by it. He's a good person."

"And he is in love with my girlfriend."

Chapter Two

Feelings

"Popcorn is my favorite." Arizona popped each kernel into his mouth like it was a delicacy, grinning as he licked buttery fingertips. His blond hair hung forward and hid his eyes. His hair was much prettier than any girl's I knew. Long and silky, it framed his tan face like a curtain when he bent his head. Then he lifted his head, and any feminine qualities ended there.

"We have more of that," my dad said. From his recliner across the room, he watched as Arizona dug around the kernels in the bottom of the jumbo-sized plastic bowl.

I imagined that Dad missed Pete, and that was the reason why he kept hanging around. Regulus and Arizona weren't the most normal guys to hang out with. I had grown up playing video games with my brother and his friends. Regulus and Arizona didn't get into gaming. Not really. They continually argued about the reality of a game scene or relayed the time that they had actually performed the feat in real life.

So, we watched movies, and I taught them poker. Tonight, Dad had rented an action flick, and he'd brought a chick flick for me. When he'd asked the guys if they wanted to watch the movies, they'd immediately said yes. The action movie was great, and they both enjoyed it. The chick flick was in the player for ten minutes when Dad got up.

"That's it for me. I'm done for the night." He rose from his chair to head upstairs. "Make sure you lock up and turn the alarm on." He turned out the kitchen light before pausing at the stairs. "Good night everybody. You guys drive safely when you head back to the dorm."

"Yes, sir. We will do that," Regulus answered from his spot a foot away from me on the sofa.

"Thanks for the snacks," Arizona added.

I turned to see Dad's feet disappear up the stairs. The movie was not one that I would have picked. Cute guy meets perfect girl. They fall in love within minutes and then the roadblocks pop up. Regulus appeared to be mesmerized.

"We don't have to watch this." I scooted closer to him on the sofa. He leaned his head back, looking tired. He put his hand out, palm up, inviting me to place mine in his.

"I'm going to go on back. I'm getting sleepy." Arizona yawned with his arms stretched above his head. He smiled then, and I knew that he was performing.

"See ya later, Arizona." I grinned back at him,

knowing that he was trying to give us time alone.

He let himself out, and I heard the motorcycle start and then pull away from the house. Leaning my head on Regulus's shoulder, I exhaled deeply, contented.

Regulus rubbed his thumb across my knuckles before holding it to his lips.

A strange tingly sensation zipped through my body, and I caught my breath in anticipation. Tightly strung, I swayed closer to his shoulder and twisted to face him. He smelled of the woods. The scent of cedar and pine from his clothing filled my nose and translated to me as a warm yellow glow. He always filled me with warmth and happiness. I leaned in to nuzzle his neck.

"Your father."

"Hmm. He sleeps like a log."

"He will not like this if he walks down here."

"He doesn't sleepwalk," I whispered with my eyes closed.

Regulus slid his hand to the back of my hair. He drew me closer, and then we kissed. A slow easy kiss at first, and then as the pressure increased, so did my heart rate. He let go of my hand, and I clutched his shoulders.

He pulled away. "What comes next for us, Mia?"

"What do you mean?"

"I think you know what I am asking. This kissing is nice, but it is a catalyst."

"A catalyst?" I sat in stunned silence. "I'll never get used to your way of putting something that's supposed to be romantic." I scooted away several inches to sit with my arms folded, tracing patterns on the knee of my jeans. I could hear his breathing in the quiet room. Out of the corner of my eye, I saw him lean his head back on the sofa to stare at the ceiling.

"My conversation will never be romantic. You know who I am. My language skills are expert level but not native."

"I wasn't really complaining about your language skills." I glanced up at him. "You don't ever talk about your feelings."

Regulus sighed.

The sound surprised me. At least it showed a level of frustration, and that was better than nothing. I touched his arm, but he continued to stare at the ceiling.

"I yearn for you. Does it make you happy to hear that? I think about your touch and your body when I need to focus on the duties I have been given." His voice came across flat and uncaring, but the words gave me chills.

"Arizona said something about being in lust. It's more than that, right?" I wished he would look at me.

"Arizona says too much."

"You're not denying it."

"All people our age lust. It is a physiological reaction."

"What if I said I didn't?"

"You would be lying." He chose that moment to look into my eyes.

He was right.

"I think I need to go to bed. It's getting late."

"If I were Arizona, I would ask to join you. But I am not. He knows the way to flirt with a girl by saying the things that make them giggle. I say what I know is true. I'm sorry if the truth makes you upset."

"I want the truth. And I'm fine with the way you are honest about...everything."

"Then it is time for me to say good night. Your father will be awake upstairs and listening for me to leave. He will be glad when he hears my motorcycle start. I may not know everything about the dating rituals here, but I do know one thing. Your dad is very afraid that our physical relationship will progress too far."

"Ugh. This conversation is beginning to freak me out. I would rather not hear about my dad and sex in the same sentence."

"I said nothing about sex in that sentence, Mia. See...you do have it on your mind."

And then he laughed. Relief flooded through me that he wasn't mad.

* * *

"Why does it bother you? Most guys don't like to talk about their emotions. It's a guy thing." Em's persuasive voice soothed me across the phone line. Her warm tone of voice always filled my head with a pink rush of color.

I tucked another pillow underneath my head. "I wonder if he's had lots of girlfriends in the past." I chewed on the edge of my thumbnail and moved the cell phone to the other ear.

"Probably," she said. "Look at him. I mean, you

know how some poor guy might have been hit with the ugly stick? He was hit with the gorgeous stick."

I snorted. "That is the most ridiculous thing I've ever heard."

"Uh-huh. Scale of one to ten. Come on...I think he's a nine point nine. Right?"

"You shouldn't be rating my boyfriend." I attempted to sound indignant. I failed miserably.

"I'm just saying that he's really fine. And he's not an idiot. And he's built like he plays soccer or does extreme sports—"

"He does extreme sports. Working for the IIA isn't for wimps."

"Tell me again what that stands for?"

"Interdimensional Immigration Authorities," I answered.

"Do they have some kind of entrance exam that requires you look like that?"

"Maybe," I said, laughing. "That would explain why he and Arizona both look that way."

Silence filled the phone line.

"Do you want to talk about Arizona?"

"Not really."

I waited for more. When none came, I decided to force the issue. "Look. It's obvious that Arizona flirts his head off with you, and then you flirt back. To a degree. But then other times you act...well...like he's the plague."

"I do not." Em denied the accusation, but her response was weak. She cleared her throat. "Flirt with him."

"There's nothing wrong with that, Em."

"I know that." Her voice filled with defensive vibes.

"Listen, I've gotta go."

Her quick exit line worried me. Usually we talked for at least an hour and the call ended only if I had to leave. Em liked to talk to me on the phone. It prevented her mom from nagging at her about being better at school, sports, or being the perfect daughter.

"I'll talk to you tomorrow then." I reluctantly let her off the hook.

* * *

I woke from a dream about my mother. I never thought about her in my waking hours, but she had a habit of sneaking into my dreams.

I was a small girl again. The funny thing was, she hadn't been around during that time. The woman had left when I was a toddler, which was good because I didn't really remember her. Or miss her. Not really.

With my knees tucked under my chin, I tried to recall the events of the dream. Something nagged at the edge of my consciousness and swirled around. I closed my eyes tightly and attempted to see the dream behind the dark curtain of my lids, but there was nothing.

Like the answer that comes from nowhere during a pop quiz, I visualized a brown cardboard box. The flaps on the sides were lifted, and the woman put items into the box. I watched a replay of the items moving from her hands to the box. Baby clothes and a photo album floated into the box. The hands shook as they moved to close the box's flaps.

I jumped from my bed and grabbed a fleece robe. Sticking my arms into the sleeves, I blindly inserted my feet into house slippers and held my breath as I cracked the bedroom door and peered into the hallway.

Anticipating Biscuit's bark, I told him, "Shh..." I could feel him at my feet since he thought he had to follow me everywhere. His usual exuberance was absent in the early morning hours, and he trotted within inches of me down the stairs. After turning off the alarm to the right of the door, I crept to the kitchen where I could exit to the garage.

Two spotlights hanging on the roof corners lit the garage door. I didn't open the large, vehicle-entry door but went to the side door. Reaching underneath a fake plastic stone, I found the hidden key and entered.

Biscuit followed me inside the garage, cheerfully wagging his tail and running his nose along the edges of all the boxes. I turned on the light and looked around. What was in all these boxes? I began to tear the seal on the first unmarked cardboard box. Sitting cross-legged on the chilly concrete floor, I removed the first mystery from within while Biscuit sat and nuzzled his nose into the small of my back.

Sliding my fingers along the edges of a silver picture frame, I gingerly separated it from the other contents of the box. The five-by-seven was new to me. I had seen only a few pictures in our house like the one I held.

The close-up of the woman captured her from the

waist up. Her arms were stretched high to hold an infant above her head. The baby wore no clothes and stared straight into the woman's eyes. Although naked, the side view didn't tell me if it was a boy or girl, this baby with a downy cap of blond hair and dark eyes. The expression on the woman's face interested me most of all. Pure delight radiated from her wide smile to her shining eyes. Crinkles at the corners of her eyes hinted at laughter. I looked at her face and found my mouth filled with the sweet tastes of vanilla and sugar. The warmth of it frustrated me. I knew the truth.

I tossed the picture onto the top of the next stack of cardboard boxes. Reaching into the box, I took out a soft, pastel-colored square—a green and yellow baby blanket. I refolded it and tucked it away. The last thing I wanted was for my dad to see that I had gone through any of the boxes.

Below the blanket, I carefully unwrapped the first of several newspapered items. I held a pink ceramic pig and tilted it, listening to the musical clink of coins in its belly. After unwrapping another package, I marveled at the weight of the tiny silver box monogrammed with a scripted "M." I pried the lid off, then gasped when a tiny tooth tumbled out and fell to my feet. I hurriedly retrieved it, replacing it in the box. Next, I extracted a Ziploc bag with a tiny pink brush with pliable bristles, nail clippers, and several pacifiers.

The last item in the box was a scrapbook, with pink lambs on its cover. The title was *Baby Memories*. I sat cross-legged with it in my lap. I opened it to the first page, then read the inscription.

Name: *Mia Carina Taylor*
Parents: *Steven and Nancy Taylor*
The print was simple and neat.

My heart raced at the implications that she had actually claimed me once. I turned all the pages, resting on several to read a journal-type entry recounting a first smile, sitting up, and doctor visits.

An indescribable anger filled me. How could she have written these things as if they'd mattered? The bitter taste of truth forced me to swallow hard. I couldn't understand this person holding the baby in the picture. How had she changed from the smiling woman to the one I had met with a gun in her hand?

I replaced the book in the box and closed the flaps. The box had raised more questions, not revealed answers. Biscuit followed me quietly out of the garage and away from the memories.

* * *

The knock at the door startled me. I ran to the window and parted the sheer curtain to see two motorcycles parked in the drive. Swinging the front door open, I eyed them both suspiciously.

"What's going on? I didn't expect to see you this early." I glanced at my watch. Eight o'clock on a Sunday morning. Most would think that company knocking at the door at this hour on a weekend was weird, but I was getting used to the weird and unexpected.

"Come on in," I said. I smiled to take the edge off

my earlier greeting. I took Regulus's hand and yanked him inside. I rubbed his cold hand between both of mine. Arizona followed, immediately making himself at home by removing his heavy jacket.

"We have something important to do today and thought you might be interested in tagging along." Regulus looked around—for my dad, I guess—and when he was satisfied we were alone, he said, "You have some training to begin."

"No one ever told me about any training." I imagined running through tires and doing push-ups. I frowned.

"We'll take advantage of the talents that we've already witnessed. Marksmanship, problem solving, portal detection...nothing too outside your range of abilities. And we'll work on the things you don't do well, like following my orders." Regulus paced around the room like he had unspent energy that needed releasing.

"I'd like to work on her cooking skills. I'm starved." Arizona said it with mock seriousness.

I playfully hit him on the arm. "You're always hungry. I swear you're a bottomless pit." I waved for them to follow me into the kitchen. They both took seats at the heavy oak dining table while I began opening cabinet doors in search of something quick and easy.

"What about the eggs and bacon your father made last weekend?" Arizona looked around at the countertops like the food would magically appear. "That was very tasty."

"Yes, I'm sure you thought so." I laughed at his sad expression. "But since I've never done that, you might get lucky enough to get a Pop-Tart or cereal." I grabbed some bananas and oranges from the fruit bowl on the counter and put them on the table.

"Where's your father?" Regulus asked. He grabbed an orange while Arizona slid the bowl across the table and examined the cereal boxes. Regulus scored the rind with a pocketknife so that he circled the circumference from top to bottom. Then he peeled off exact sections to place on a paper towel. The precise, surgical method of eating an orange was very much like him.

"I forget," I said. "He got up really early and said good-bye before he left. He flew out to somewhere on the East Coast."

"And when will he be back?" Regulus nodded, looking pleased.

"End of the week," I said. "Thursday or Friday. I can't remember. I guess I don't pay attention."

"You should. It is an important detail." Regulus's voice held a scolding tone that irritated me. I was the most responsible teenager in Whispering Woods.

"Well, um-hum. Is something going on in my so-called training at the end of the week? If you expect me to be strategically planning my schedule, it would be nice to clue me in."

"It is important because he is your father. No other reason according to Arizona," Regulus said.

Arizona poured cereal into his bowl and helped himself to milk from the refrigerator. His chomping sounded overly loud in the next few moments. He always kept quiet when I wished he would jump in and take one side or the other. He smiled at me. "I've been explaining some family issues to Regulus this morning."

"Huh?" My irritation subsided, replaced by confusion. I put bread into the toaster. "What kind of family issues?" I asked suspiciously.

"Role of a father. Although I didn't know mine until I was older, I had one. Before my father came to get me, I had several men who acted as a father. I basically know how it works," Arizona said matter-of-factly. He rose and went to the counter, reaching for the bread.

I glanced at Regulus and wondered what Arizona had told him. He had finished the peeled orange and was spinning a whole one like it was a top.

"The father is different from the mother in the nurturing of an offspring," Regulus said it like he was reciting from a book. "He shows affection for the offspring in a different manner as his biological makeup demands protection of family."

"My dad loves me just because." My words came out simple and childlike. "I'm all he has right now."

"And when you leave him?" Regulus asked.

"Why would I leave? I mean, sure I'll leave someday after college. I'll probably still see him at least once a week, even then," I said.

"I don't understand these parental attachments, but I'm trying to learn them," Regulus said. "What do you know of your mother?"

"Coldhearted witch." The answer was simple to me.

"But Steven Taylor had emotional ties with this woman." Regulus rose and crossed the room to stare at the picture on the refrigerator. Most of the four-by-six prints were of Peter and me. A few included my dad. Regulus picked through the numerous photos until he found the one he wanted. "Do you have memories of this woman?"

He held the one picture that I'd hidden beneath the others. I hadn't thrown it away because I knew Pete would've been angry if he returned to find it missing. The family portrait was covered by several other pictures and magnets. The section of the picture with the woman holding the baby had been covered. I wasn't sure how Regulus had discovered it.

"No, not really." I thought about my midnight trip to the garage and the dream that had prompted my curiosity. "She left us and went to start a new life somewhere. It was a long time ago."

Arizona stopped crunching the cereal. "How do you know that was your mother that you saw in Dr. Bleeker's house?"

"It was Nancy Taylor," Regulus said flatly.

Arizona and I both stared at Regulus. He obviously had information about the woman who had been missing from my life the last fifteen years.

"What do you know that we don't? I thought it was her, but I wasn't sure." I accused him with my tone. I waited for him to look guilty, but he didn't look apologetic at all.

Over a month ago, Regulus and I had searched an empty house looking for Dr. Bleeker. Instead, we'd been surprised by two people, a man and woman, who seemed to be intent on killing us. Or that was my interpretation of the gun aimed at the back of my head. The woman had been Nancy Taylor, my mother.

"I know of your mother. I have reviewed a file of your entire family." Regulus always met my gaze when he talked. His unwavering blue eyes never held any regret or avoidance.

When I got nervous, I couldn't meet those eyes. I ended up looking at the small, almost imperceptible dimple in his chin. "What did you learn that makes you positive that it was her? A lot of women look like the one we saw. Blonde, petite, pretty."

"Nancy Taylor has a scar along her right cheek. She also has a condition called heterochromia."

I didn't want to ask what it meant. It sounded like some horrible disease. After waiting a moment for an explanation, I decided to ask. "I give. What is that?"

"One green eye and one blue," Regulus answered.

"You noticed all that in the few minutes we saw her?" My mouth dropped open in amazement. I couldn't tell you what the woman was wearing, much less the color of her eyes. My mind had been racing with the problem of her gun to my head. And how to save myself and Regulus from biting the dust in Bleeker's house.

"You said that you thought it was your mother as we walked out of Dr. Bleeker's home," Regulus said. "Then we have a positive identification, correct?"

I shrugged. "Your guess is as good as mine. I hope we've seen the last of her."

Now close to me, Regulus murmured, "You know that we will meet her again. She is a traitor. She may be involved in the disappearance of your brother."

The pounding of my heart sounded in my ears. I could hear my own breathing in the silence that followed. My hatred for her grew to an incomprehensible level.

"Stop keeping information from me. What makes you think that she had anything to do with Pete leaving?" I waited for Regulus to respond. He was silent, to my chagrin. "What's in the file? My mother left when I was only a baby. She's living with some new family somewhere in Idaho or Nebraska. Or maybe Alaska..." My childish protests sounded weak.

Regulus rubbed my shoulder, comforting me before he moved away. Had he remembered Arizona was watching? "Your mother was an agent of the IIA. That is how I know these things. You have the gifts that your mother passed to you. Genetic gifts. She was a synesthete."

His gentleness made my throat constrict. I stared at the pictures on the refrigerator door.

"Do you miss this woman? Your mother?" he asked.

"No, I don't know Nancy. But I can tell you that she has never been a mother to me." I drew a deep breath. "We need to find her as well, right? And turn her over to the IIA." I glanced from Regulus to Arizona for confirmation. Neither one would look at me.

"I wish it were that easy," Regulus said. "We are not authorized to bring Nancy Taylor to the IIA. She has been granted autonomy. She is a citizen here."

"The woman put a gun to my head...her own daughter. I don't get it. We're supposed to bring Bleeker in, but you can't turn that woman into them? That doesn't make sense."

"Bleeker doesn't belong here. He is not an original

citizen and was never granted the right to live here. Nancy Taylor must stay here. She belongs here no matter what illegal activities she is performing. Your government has jurisdiction over her."

"I don't care. If she knows something about Pete, then I'll find her too." I lifted my chin. "I could do a citizen's arrest. That's my right." My skewed logic probably wouldn't get me anywhere, but I was desperate. My voice had risen, and I stood, glaring at Regulus, challenging him.

"What about your high-school winter formal? Are you taking Regulus, and does Emily have a date?" Arizona asked.

Regulus and I both swiveled to face him.

"How do you know about that?" I sputtered in confusion. The shift in conversation threw me.

Arizona grinned like a Cheshire cat. "I listen. Emily talked with you about girls getting asked by certain boys. I'm interested in how this works."

"I don't think I'll go." I avoided looking at either one of them.

"Regulus will take you," Arizona said as he grinned at Regulus.

Silence.

"It's not a big deal. Really." The words were rushing out of my mouth of their own volition. "I don't go to most of these things anyway. It's all about clothes and who's taking who, and it will probably be lame because I've heard the original deejay has canceled and now they're looking for a band instead of a deejay—"

"Yes," Regulus said. "I want to take you. Unless there is some reason you don't want me to go."

"I..." I finally looked up into his eyes. "You don't have to go. It's a stupid high-school thing. Really stupid."

"I said I would like to go. You must tell me the rules for it." He seemed uncertain all of a sudden. "Am I not requesting it properly?"

"There aren't a lot of rules. You've asked fine," I said. I wanted the awkwardness to go away. "Yeah. I'd like to go with you." As an afterthought, I added, "You'll have to wear something different from your everyday clothes. There's a store on the square downtown that has tuxes. You could wear a tux, if you want to." I shrugged, my face heating. I really hadn't planned to go.

"And Emily. Would Emily go with me if I asked her?" Arizona asked, looking very pleased. I didn't know how he had shifted the conversation away from my issues with a renegade mother to this, but he had.

"I can't answer that. But I think she might. Maybe." I had a hard time figuring out where Arizona stood with Emily. I didn't want to give him false hope.

"Good," Arizona said. "I'll call her later. Now, we go to the woods for training."

Chapter Three

Fight Training

"Portal finder. I can do that. I didn't sign up for this other part." I shivered in the cold morning. Deep in the woods, a fine mist hung in the damp, sticky air. We had walked at a brisk pace to match Regulus's for a couple of miles, and now my hair clung to my neck and cheeks. Irritated, I shoved the strands off my face.

"These skills are necessary for all agents of the IIA, portal finder or not." Regulus nodded at Arizona. "Arizona is adept in judo, jujitsu, and several other martial arts. He is small but quick."

I looked at Arizona, a head taller than myself.

"I am skilled in everything from hand-to-hand combat to weaponry. You do not have time to become skilled in anything," Regulus said.

"Gee, thanks," I answered.

"You will rely on your ability in marksmanship,

which you recently demonstrated irresponsibly."
Regulus referred to an incident over a month ago at
Dr. Bleeker's involving a gun and a precise shot into
the thigh of a bad guy holding Regulus. Video gaming
had paid off for once.

Arizona smirked. "I think she did pretty well.
Saved your backside," he said.

Regulus shot him a look that would wilt most
people, but Arizona grinned even wider. Then he took
off his backpack and removed two weapons, setting
them in a precise line on the ground: a black-
handled, five-inch-long knife, and the silver box from
Regulus's world that I called a stunner.

Examining the knife, I imagined slitting someone
with it. Nah. The knife wasn't my style. I picked up
the stunner.

"Be careful," Regulus said as if I were a child. "You
could hurt yourself."

"Do I finally get one of these?" I asked the question
and then stuck out my tongue at him. The wind blew
and twirled leaves around my head in a kaleidoscope
of red and orange. I pushed hair out of my eyes.

"This is how you hold it." Regulus took the
rectangular box from me with deliberate care. He
held it much like a cell phone and said, "Make
certain that the opaque end faces out." He then
pointed somewhere in the distance. "See that tree
with the knot in the center?"

I shook my head.

"I will take the limb off. The one that is a foot above
our heads." Regulus pointed the stunner and
squeezed both sides. A high-pitched whistle
sounded, and the tree limb fell to the ground. "Now,

you shall hold it. No pressure should be exerted in this hold." He handed me the box. "Hold it lightly."

I studied the object in my palm that I'd held in the past without a clue as to its inner workings. The sides were malleable with a gel-like quality. Anxious, I tried not to squeeze. A mockingbird chattered and startled me into a jittery bundle of nerves.

"What makes it go off?" I asked.

"You do," Regulus said. "Now you will exert pressure with your thumb and forefinger and tell it to discharge."

"Tell it?" I shifted uncomfortably at the thought of talking to the stunner. Regulus hadn't done that. I raised my eyebrows, unsure that I had heard him correctly.

"You can do it with your voice, but it isn't necessary. Direct the command with your mind." Regulus nodded his head toward the tree. "This is going to take all morning if you must question everything that I tell you to do."

Arizona had carried a sword into the woods and began executing slicing motions parallel to his body. Ever since we had taken the sword from Ms. Amazon, he had been obsessed with it. He ignored us.

"I don't get it. Where is the trigger? My voice?"

"Stop talking." Regulus stood behind my shoulder and brought his arm forward, covering my hand with his. "Hold it like a gun. Steady."

"Nothing is happening." I pressed with my thumb and finger.

"Close your eyes," he whispered. "Think about the discharge and mentally tell the weapon to obey. Be certain that your fingers make firm contact."

For once, I didn't argue. I concentrated on the weight of the weapon in my hand and pressed while I wished for it to fire. I heard the faint whistling sound and opened my eyes to see what I had done. Nothing looked different. If a branch had fallen, I couldn't tell.

One hundred yards away to the left, an ancient oak tree bent in half and popped in protest. Several jolting shrugs later, the top five feet bent at a forty-five degree angle and creaked as it drooped toward the ground. A displaced flock of birds chattered while settling in another treetop.

Arizona chuckled to himself without making a comment.

Regulus rubbed his hand over the back of his neck. "I think you have it. Now let's try with the eyes open. But this time, think less forcefully. It may be important to keep the landscape intact, and there is a rather small mountain over there quivering in fear." A slight smile tugged at the corner of his mouth.

"This is too sweet. It's superhero stuff, in case you didn't know. No Slip will ever mess with me again."

"This weapon is mine. I'm only showing you how to use it. It's too dangerous for you to have one in your possession." Regulus almost sounded sorry.

"That's not fair. Why tease me with it?" My shoulders slumped as I looked around for a target.

Regulus took the stunner from my hand. "You may get your own some day. For now, you can use mine in case of emergency."

"Great. I'm feeling as though I'm five years old.

Want to just hand me a pointy stick and hope I can defend myself?" I glanced down. "I do get the knife, right?"

"A pointy stick might be best for you and your impulsiveness, but yes, you will use the knife." Regulus's mouth was a straight, hard line. "You will use the weapon from a distance for now. You have demonstrated very good aim in the past."

He touched my hair, then strode over to a tree some distance away and removed a sheet of paper from his pocket.

Frustrated, I watched. He vacillated between shyness and boldness, and I rarely knew where I stood with him.

When he backed up, I could see his work. The paper was attached to the tree. Staring at the bull's-eye target, I muttered, "You expect me to hit that? With the knife? You're kidding, right?"

Returning, he handed me the knife by the handle. "First you place your right foot in the back. Then your feet should be approximately two feet apart." He reached over to move my left leg into position. Then, he demonstrated how to place my feet.

"Can I throw it now?" I asked impatiently.

"Bend your knees." His voice was even, as always. He took the knife from my hand. "I will demonstrate first. I should have thought of that."

He assumed the stance he had taught me and extended both arms in front of his body. He quickly looped back his right arm, then shifted his body as he flung the knife so fast I didn't see his right hand release it. The blade whizzed through the air and struck the center of the bull's-eye, pinning the target.

Arizona had stopped practicing with the sword to watch. He jogged to the tree and tugged out the knife. Strolling back, he remarked, "We could let her use something easier."

"No," I said, peevish. "Don't make allowances for me. I can do this."

I eyed the knife for a second and then took it from Arizona. Though smooth, the handle was too large, awkward. When my posture and footing looked correct and balanced, I drew my arms forward as I'd been shown. I wound back my right arm as fast as I could and threw the knife. It went sailing through the air to fall...somewhere. Past the tree.

Regulus stared at the tree trunk.

Arizona ran forward to find the knife. He hunted through the piles of dead leaves before spotting it. Trotting back, he returned it to me. "That wasn't terrible. It even landed somewhat near the tree."

"Thanks," I said. "I'm sure a bad guy will run when I throw a knife within four feet of him."

"Again," Regulus said softly with no apparent expectation that I would argue.

We continued in the fruitless exercise until my arm began to hurt, and I needed a bathroom break. I wanted to go back home and crawl back into my warm bed. Clouds had gathered overhead and a chill pervaded the clearing. My woolly sweater didn't provide the heat I needed in spite of the exercise.

"Can we go in now? Lunch maybe?" I looked at Arizona since he would be easier to bait with a meal. I widened my eyes innocently. "Sure could use a burger."

"You would cook us hamburgers?" Arizona sounded hopeful.

I almost felt guilty.

Regulus looked from my face to Arizona's. "Your arm is weak. Yes, we will stop."

"My arm is not weak. I can't help it if repeating the same motion fifty times is causing muscle fatigue." I handed him the knife. "I told you that I didn't sign up for this part." I smiled at him. "Find Pete, chill with you guys, locate a portal or two, save the world from hazardous baddies. If I can find Pete, my work here is done."

"I envy you." Regulus stated the words with honesty. "It must be pleasant to be carefree of the responsibilities you should carry. Has it occurred to you that you could be saving your people, your world, from extinction?"

"I think you're exaggerating a little. Don't you?" I asked gently. Dr. Bleeker had killed test subjects. Serious, but he wasn't purposely killing all humans.

"Your earth's role as our seed vault calls for extreme measures to ensure its safety," Regulus explained with a shrug. "I do not see how you can be blind to the severity of this situation."

After a few moments of gathering the equipment Arizona had brought to the woods, he finally spoke. "She can't be blamed for her innocence. Not everyone has been trained in the enlightenment of interdimensional existence."

"Who trained you in this…enlightenment?" I asked Arizona since he was originally from this world. I had a picture in my mind of a military spaceship with recruits standing in a row. Their blue uniforms would have shiny black buttons to match their boots. I laughed when my internal vision panned to Arizona in the line with his surfer blond hair and constant grin.

"The IIA, of course. And I've learned a lot from Regulus. He was my mentor for assimilation when I was twelve." Arizona said the words with a hint of gratitude, and Regulus looked uncomfortable.

I looked to Regulus. "Teach me then."

Regulus shook his head. "It's worse with you than it was with Arizona. You argue with everything I say."

"And he didn't argue," I said in understanding.

"No, because we came to an agreement." Arizona smiled widely as he said it. "Because when I was brought in seven years ago, the IIA placed me in the Vault to live. Regulus slept in the bunk below mine and was assigned to me as a mentor even though we're the same age."

Regulus laughed, a low rumble emanating from his chest. "I was not happy with the assignment. Arizona had a difficult time understanding that rules are to be followed."

"And you follow all the rules, right?" I asked.

"Apparently not." Arizona grinned at Regulus. "Level A misdemeanor for an agent to engage in romantic activities with a citizen of another dimension he is patrolling."

"Level A? What does that mean?"

Regulus glared at Arizona. "Nothing really."

"It has to mean something. Don't brush off my question. I know that you aren't supposed to be dating me." I felt funny calling it dating since all we ever did was hang out with Arizona or my friends.

We had very little time alone.

Arizona shuffled his feet uncomfortably. "You should tell her. She has a right to know since she is now one of us."

"She's not one of us," Regulus said.

"Oh, that's so not all right. I'm either on this team or not." I couldn't imagine what could be so bad. I hugged my arms tightly around my body. I followed Regulus and Arizona as they began to hike through the woods, but walking wouldn't stop my questions.

"The Council would determine the best course of action." Regulus spoke quietly as if someone might overhear. He stopped to rearrange his backpack before he spoke again. "Most times, Level A for this type of criminal behavior is a reprogram."

My mouth dropped open at the term criminal behavior. "It's not criminal. And what do you mean by reprogram?" My voice echoed in the woods. I searched Regulus's expressionless face before I glanced at Arizona, searching for clues in his features.

"Memory cleanse," Regulus said in a neutral manner.

"The IIA cleans your memory? You mean that they'd make you forget me?" My voice rose shrilly and ended in a tiny squeak. I grabbed Regulus's arm, forcing him to stop.

"It is not possible for them to learn of us. If I believed the risk to be too high, I would tell you." Regulus's deep blue eyes met mine before he looked away and shrugged dismissively.

I shook my head in disbelief.

"Arizona does this all the time." Regulus's remark

was so unlike him that I stared from one to the other.

"And you've never worried about getting caught?" I asked Arizona. I began to walk again, matching their strides. Maybe I was overreacting after all.

"If they wiped a romantic encounter or a person from my memory, it would be unfortunate, but not fatal." Arizona laughed at his own joke. On seeing my expression, he added, "I think it's worth the risk, Mia. The worst that can happen is that you wouldn't remember those feelings or the person."

"The worst that could happen..." I kept walking.

* * *

Em sat at my desktop computer while I shoved dirty clothes into a portable hamper. I hated doing laundry more than any other chore. Most kids my age had a mom around to do laundry, producing nicely ironed shirts and replacing missing buttons. I'd been doing my laundry since I was six years old. A few loads of turning all my clothes pink from the red shirt that slipped in, and I'd decided to become a sorting expert. Still, I put off laundry day as long as possible.

Em, who could focus like a brain surgeon, ignored me as I sorted my pieces into two hampers. I marveled at her ability to see the details in a picture. *Where's Waldo* had always been a walk in the park for her. As I scooted behind her shoulder to read her notes, I noticed her eyes scanned the picture from left to right as if she were reading though the picture had no text.

"What are you looking for?" I sat on a stool beside her. I couldn't fathom what a person could learn from the sea of faces I saw on-screen.

"Similarities. Differences. Things that don't belong." She blew a wisp of perfect, blonde bangs from her eyes. Her hair was done in a style framing her pretty face but nearly hiding it. I always brushed my hair back in a ponytail so it wouldn't obstruct my view. Practicality always won out over fashion.

"I don't see anything." I leaned in as if a closer view would help.

Em clicked to freeze the video frame. She then magnified on a group of people and I saw my face and hers come into view. "Take these two, for instance. The taller girl is looking around for something while her friend is talking to her. Obviously not paying attention to an important conversation."

I sighed and looked at the two people on the screen, me and Em. Austin stood slightly over to the side. I was a lot taller than Em and dressed my usual T-shirt with jeans. Em wore a short skirt and long matching top that screamed "mall purchase." Standing side-by-side we illustrated contrast.

"We don't even look like we came from the same planet. That's what I see. Two girls who don't match." I smiled to take the edge off the words. "You look ready to hit the runway, and I look like I'm on the run."

"Not hardly." Em twisted her thumb ring and tilted her head before shaking her head in denial. She turned back to the screen. "Same blonde hair, same age, standing close together. I'm leaning in talking to you, so a person could guess we know each other. Lots of similarities. Differences? I look like I'm having fun and you look unhappy. Maybe not that. You look distracted like you are looking for someone or something. "

"See that guy? He's the one who was obnoxious in that session on setting up a tournament. I hate gum smackers." I bobbed my head.

"This guy here is the one you thought was following you." She touched the computer monitor, resting her finger on his head.

"He was following me, Em."

"That's what I meant. Anyway, here's the one I noticed." She pointed at a person holding a camera. The man looked through what appeared to be something more than a regular digital camera. The lens was extended for magnification at a distance.

"The camera lens is pointed at Pete over here. See?" Em stared at me to see my reaction.

"Oh." The implications of this new discovery raced through my mind. "He was looking for Pete." I sat on the bed and watched Em use a software drawing tool to circle the screen around the man in question.

"Were they looking at Pete because they knew you would be there, or was it the other way around? There are some more people in this video to study. Here's someone who's obviously people watching and that would be normal with the flash mob." Em stopped the video again before continuing. She clicked a still frame of the image and drew another circle.

"How do you know he isn't someone who was there

for the conference?"

"No conference bag. It had lots of goodies from the vendor. We paid enough for it. Can you believe that we got a promo game from Celeron Dreams? I played it last night."

"The guy, Em? What about the guy?"

She smiled. "Sorry. He isn't carrying a bag, and while it's possible that he decided he didn't want to hang onto it, it's unlikely. Deduction? He's a bad guy out scanning the crowd for you. Or Pete."

"I can buy that."

"The question is why Pete if not you?" Em tilted her head to look over her shoulder.

"He's on the run from someone. It has to be these people. My instincts tell me that this is still tied to Dr. Bleeker."

"You can assume that, but we don't know for sure. Please don't get mad at me for what I'm about to say." Em stopped talking and waited for my response.

"Go on."

"No, promise me that you will consider this without getting all excited."

"OK. You have my word." I had no idea what would bring on this degree of concern.

"What if it is someone looking for Pete, someone besides Bleeker...since we thought he would only be looking for you. We know the IIA wanted Pete for their own purposes. What if he is running from them?"

"Regulus and Arizona have nothing to do with the thugs who followed us around at GameCon." My hackles were up before I could stop my reaction. I saw from Em's face that she expected as much. "Em,

Regulus almost died from the trap that somebody set at my house while I was gone to GameCon. You know that."

"Right. But could it be possible that Dr. Bleeker set the trap? And the IIA didn't send Regulus and Arizona, but other agents, to Dallas?" Em waited for me to soak in the possibility before speaking again. "I'm not saying that this is what I think. I think it is a possibility."

My breath stuck in my throat as I thought about Regulus and his trust for the IIA. I believed with every cell in my body that Regulus was sure he worked for the good guys. "I'm trying to stay open-minded. If Pete is running from the IIA, I'm sure that Regulus doesn't know."

Em started the video again and located two other men she circled on-screen with the drawing tool. She clicked on the Stop button and glanced sideways at me. "I'm not saying that I think Regulus knew anything about it. I know you're in deep." She leaned back in the chair as far as she could go without falling over.

I flopped belly first on top of my bed and rested my chin on my folded hands. "I've never really cared about boyfriends...or lack of."

"Um-hum." Em withdrew a bottle of nail polish from her bag and waved it. "You mind?"

"Go ahead."

"And now you're worried about boyfriends, now that you have one? Where is this going?"

"I'm torn between wanting to know Regulus better and being scared of knowing him better. He drives me crazy. I think about him all the time. But when we're together, it gets complicated. Most of the time, he only talks about the IIA and training me."

"That's all you do together?" Em grinned because she knew the answer.

"No. We do other things," I answered hesitantly.

"Your relationship sounds normal to me."

"If we aren't talking about the IIA and finding Dr. Bleeker, we're...you know...kissing."

"So what's the problem?"

"There's so much that I don't know about him. And he knows everything about me. Too much. They have a file on my entire family."

"You ever read the file?"

"No."

"Then how do you know that it's everything?"

"I don't. But he knows stuff about my mother." Silence. The topic was always uncomfortable. Em's mother was the type who overpowered her life. Mine had conveniently disappeared when I was a toddler. They were both unspoken burdens in our psyches.

"What did he tell you?" Emily asked in a near whisper, her hand poised above the last toenail she was painting. She was holding her breath.

I focused on the brush in her hand. The polish was pink and glittery. "I guess she was a synesthete like me."

"Is that all he said?"

"No, he knows what she looks like." I met her eyes. "He said she has a scar on her right cheek. My mother has eyes of two colors—one green and one blue."

"You didn't know that?"

"No, I didn't." I sounded angry and exasperated.

"Sorry. I don't remember much about her. I've seen a few pictures. But when I look at them, I see her face and I think about what she did to us... Leaving her husband and two kids... I never look at her eyes."

"Why did she leave...if you don't mind me asking?"

"I really don't know. I'm sure that dad is better off without her. She put a gun to my head the last time I saw her."

Em didn't appreciate my sarcasm. "Did she recognize you? You've grown up since then." She leaned forward and put her hand on my shoulder. "She would have to be a monster if she remembers you and still did what she did."

"Like I said. Better off." I shrugged. I picked up a gaming magazine on my nightstand, flipping through the pages.

"What else does Regulus know?"

"That's the part that scares me. What's worse...not knowing or knowing what you wish you didn't?"

Chapter Four

Austin

Austin leaned back in the chair as much as possible while examining his new ink. His shirt usually covered the tat so his mother hadn't noticed yet. The three-inch, intricate design began on his top right pec. Only someone looking for it could see the letter M on the tail of the dragon. The slight difference from the other scales on the dragon's tail was his tribute to her. Not that she would ever know about it. Grabbing the orange soda to take another swig, he shook his head in disgust.

He shoved a headset and some PlayStation game cases to the side of his desk to make room for the soda can. He glanced at the clock widget on his desktop monitor. After midnight. Closing the program on his midterm paper titled, "The Woman Question of the Victorian Age" he grimaced. It would be nice to understand the women of this decade.

He clicked on the *Quest of Zion* icon, logged in, and

waited. The startup screen tended to annoy him. He wished the programmers would add the skip link he'd requested. He opened a cellophane package of chocolate-covered espresso beans and popped a couple into his mouth.

Online users filled the right frame of his screen, and he closed the extra frame. Most of his friends played during this time, but he didn't feel like chatting. He clicked on the link to his private game area that he and some of his hardcore gaming friends used. Tiny was already playing, and Austin moved his character on the screen at a brisk pace through the virtual landscape, joining Tiny on-screen to walk beside him.

Austin reached to grab the headset he'd moved earlier and cursed as the chocolate espresso beans began rolling out of the package and along his desk. He caught and ate them. Nothing better than a good old caffeine rush to get an edge in the game. He put the headset on and positioned the mic closer to his lips. Opening the communications window, he clicked to open private talk with Tiny.

"Hey," Austin said while his on-screen stride never slowed. The character sported long blond dreadlocks that swung from side to side. Bare-chested, it looked nothing like Austin except for matching his tattoos, including the newest one on the right pec.

The second character did look exactly like his owner. The tousled red mop of curls topped the giant who towered over his companion. At six foot seven offscreen, Tiny looked down at everyone in both worlds. "What's up, man?" Tiny's voice came over the headset.

"The usual load of bull."

"Oh yeah? This have anything to do with Mia?"

"When doesn't it?" Austin's character drew an arrow from the quiver across his back. He turned forty-five degrees and shot a zombielike creature that had been following them. It fell limply to the ground with the arrow's shaft protruding from its chest. Austin's character pivoted and continued on the previous path.

Confronted by an unfriendly group and forced into battle, the two warriors retaliated. With Tiny swinging a mace and Austin a katana, they quickly defeated the motley crew while increasing the life force they collected during game play.

Spattered in blood and ready to continue on to the next checkpoint in the game, Austin was surprised by a hand on his shoulder on the opposite side from Tiny. He twisted, swinging his sword in an arc. The new character sprang nimbly to the side.

Tiny lurched forward and grabbed the character by the collar, lifting him high enough that his feet were off the ground. The stranger didn't struggle but held up both hands in surrender.

"I come in peace." The voice came over Austin's headset loud and clear.

I know that voice. Austin narrowed his eyes and leaned toward the screen. Playing in this private game required being invited by Tiny.

With his feet still six inches above ground, the stranger said calmly, "Let me down, Tiny."

Tiny dropped him.

"Is that really you, man?" Austin couldn't stop an almost imperceptible tremor as he spoke. His character pulsed, awaiting direction.

"Yeah, it's me," Pete said.

"Dude! I didn't recognize this character. Where have you been? Everybody's been looking for you. Your dad acts like he's waiting for the police to show up with a death—"

"Austin, man, hold up." Pete chuckled before his seriousness returned. "I only have a few minutes."

"Where have you been?" Tiny also wanted to know.

"Doesn't matter. What does is that Bleeker isn't far from you, and he's at it again."

"Who's Bleeker?" Tiny asked.

"Austin will have to fill you in. Hey, and Austin?" Pete said.

"Yeah." Austin turned up the volume on his audio.

"He's now taking local test subjects. Check the missing persons reports from the surrounding states. Can you do me a favor?"

"Sure," Austin said. "Whatever you need."

"I'm trying to protect Mia, but I've got a lot going on."

"Protect her from whom? Bleeker?"

"Who else would I be talking about?"

"Her new boyfriend Regulus."

"Regulus?"

"IIA dude. He and Arizona hang around your house all the time now. She's actually joined up with them."

There was a lengthy silence.

"You still there?" Austin asked.

"Processing that." Pete hesitated before continuing. "Had no idea. It's worse than I thought."

"Tell me about it." Austin grimaced.

"I'll be contacting you again. I don't want to draw attention to her from the people I work for. Can I trust you to watch out for her? You and Tiny?"

"No need to ask," Austin said.

The third character disappeared, and a message appeared in its place. *Protector has logged out.*

Chapter Five

Intruder

The glow of the night-light comforted me while I stared up at the popcorn finish on my bedroom ceiling. When I was younger, I would call Pete's name and he'd answer through the thin wall that separated our rooms. When I was older, I was calmed by the music that Pete played at night, a playlist of punk rock music that thrashed and wailed. It easily put me to sleep.

These days, the house was always quiet as a coffin. Sometimes, I could hear the television on in the den downstairs and, although I knew I should go down and turn it off, it helped me to sleep. Dad always fell asleep with the television blaring while he was at home on the weekends since he had started taking more government contracts. I liked it better when he'd worked freelance from our house.

Tonight, with Dad gone, the house creaked and

talked to me in the way houses do in the woods. Wind circled the trees, and branches pecked against the tin roof. I closed my eyes and saw a rainbow of bright, beautiful colors dancing across the room in time with nature's beat. I loved that roof. When it rained, the musical cacophony relaxed my racing mind.

A scraping sound like a metal bar skidding across my eardrum drew my attention to the dark window. The blinds were drawn, so I couldn't see if a nearby tree branch caused the noise. I sat up in bed and bent my knees to my chin. Biscuit stirred at the foot of my bed, then lunged at the window while barking ferociously.

Shards of glass fell onto my desk, and I screamed.

The miniblinds thrust forward in a warped "V" when something—someone—tried to break into my fragile security. I jumped out of bed, haphazardly grabbing for Biscuit. Although only a twelve-pound cairn terrier, my dog had Rottweiler attitude. He snarled and squirmed in my arms, trying to escape.

I stopped screaming and ran, still clinging to Biscuit. Swinging wide around the doorframe, I half tumbled down the wooden stairs. I would have traveled faster if not for the bundle of dog to balance. I could hear noise behind me and shrieked involuntarily at the thought of the intruder chasing me. The pounding of my heart matched the pounding of feet upstairs.

The thumps weren't coming any closer. I stood poised with my hand on the doorknob. My knees wobbled. Biscuit wiggled, desperate for release. Holding my breath in dread—would I see someone at the top of the stairs?—I listened to a ruckus coming from my room. Something made a shattering sound as it crashed to the floor.

I looked around for a weapon.

Running to the car would be useless since my keys sat on the dresser in my bedroom in my heart-shaped candy dish. I edged to the kitchen in the dark while still grappling with Biscuit. I knew that canisters lined the tiled length of the countertop along with a few appliances. Where were the knives? I ran one hand along the slick surface and attempted to control my breathing. Footsteps sounded from the staircase, and I frantically grabbed the first thing I could.

"It's me." The familiar voice came from the edge of the kitchen doorway seconds before I tried to smash his head in. I let my arm fall to my side and bent to release Biscuit. The dog skidded around the corner and greeted the voice's owner.

"What do you plan to do with that?" Regulus eyed the toaster in my hand. My fingers were inserted in the two slots in the top.

I hugged it to my waist. "Umm...knock you out?"

"You were going to assault the Slip with a kitchen appliance?"

"Yes," I whispered.

"You are resourceful." He glanced over his shoulder. "But you should have grabbed the knife that I gave you."

"I don't think I'm good enough with it." I frowned and stilled my shaky hands. "How did you know that someone was breaking in?"

"I constantly monitor your house. I set up a

camera exactly like you did a few months ago for your science project. Someone disabled it a few minutes ago. I knew you had to be in trouble."

"You're watching me?" My voice rose at the end involuntarily. "Exactly what part of my house are you watching?"

"The outside only, and you should be glad for it. It's the only reason I can sleep at night knowing you are out here by yourself. I thought you would be happy to see me."

"Of course I am." I set the toaster on the cabinet. The guilt of being rescued washed over me. I didn't like to feel helpless or rescued. My favorite T-shirt claimed I was a "Self-rescuing Princess," and I intended to live up to the name.

"Arizona is coming. He didn't hurry like I did."

"Thanks," I said. "For coming quickly."

"It is my job. And you had plans to incapacitate him with the kitchen appliance, right?" He shrugged his shoulders and finally smiled.

I shook my head. "I'll be ready to use a real weapon next time. I never thought anybody would break into my house."

"It is odd. Perhaps he is looking for something." Regulus said the words more to himself than to me. He began walking toward the stairs, and I followed.

The man lay face down on my bedroom floor with his outstretched hand inches away from my bed. He looked to be of average height and weight, but I still wondered how we would get him downstairs. The stunner had obviously knocked him out, and I really had no clue about how long he'd be unconscious. Regulus shared no details unless I asked him.

We rolled him over in the narrow space between the end of my bed and the wall. The intruder looked to be peacefully asleep.

"How do you know how long he's out?" I backed up slightly. A feeling of claustrophobia tightened my throat.

"I administer the hit on his nervous system according to need."

"If I had used a knife on him, there would be blood as evidence. I might have even killed him by accident. This seems much better. Why can't I have a stunner?"

"Because you can explain to the authorities that an intruder came in, and you defended yourself. You cannot explain a weapon that doesn't exist."

"Oh." It sounded logical, and I was disappointed. "Then I'll become an expert with the knife." I remembered how sore my arms had been after the practice session earlier. Grimacing, I grabbed my tennis shoes and stuck my foot into the first one. "Are we going to move this dude, or what?"

"Yes. Let us move the...dude." He smiled, and dimples appeared out of nowhere in his face. "You can hold his feet."

I nodded in agreement and watched Regulus lift the man from underneath the shoulders, slipping his hands under the armpits. Regulus linked his hands together over the guy's chest and nodded that he was ready. I lifted his feet. The guy felt like a lead weight.

The guy wore Nike tennis shoes.

"I don't think this guy is a Slip." I didn't think. I knew.

"What is making you so certain?"

"He's wearing a shoe I recognize." I struggled to keep my grip on the bottoms of the shoes as we hauled our burden. "I'd guess that people from different dimensions don't wear our shoe brands."

"That is observant of you. Anything else you see on him?" Regulus sounded slightly amused.

"He appears to have poor taste in clothes, and his cologne is overwhelming. I should have smelled him lurking outside my window." We stood at the top of the stairs with Regulus going backward down them. He waited while I adjusted my hold.

"Why do you think he's a Slip? Are the people from other dimensions like us?"

"Do I appear that different to you?" His eyebrows rose at the question.

I breathed a little harder in trying to carry the body downstairs while staying upright. "No." I had never even thought about it before. Except for his stilted speech, he seemed like an ordinary college guy to me. He was ordinary in the perfect sort of way, but not perfectly ordinary.

"My world is not far from yours. That is why we are human like you. If you have a Slip who is very different, he has come far." Regulus shifted the man's weight. "We can set him down. I hear Arizona outside."

Now at the bottom of the stairs, I gladly put the man's feet down.

"Travel is safest between the dimensions that are very close together. The physics of how atoms are held together would dictate that any farther dimensional travel would cause them to dissolve. If the dimension is not carbon based, it is not possible to exist."

"Hmmm." I didn't want to know that the world was different from what we were taught in science class. Ignorance is bliss. "What about religion? Do you believe in a creator?"

"The IIA Vault Keepers are my creator."

A shiver ran up my spine and danced around my neck. These statements from Regulus reminded me of the different worlds we knew and loved. I shook off the feeling.

I jumped at the knock on the door even though I knew Arizona was outside. But when the door opened, Austin stood with his hand on the knob. Arizona stood to his right.

"You OK, Mia?" Austin swept his dark bangs out of his eyes, worry written all over his face. "Aliens attacking your house now?" He wasn't joking like he usually did.

"I'm fine, Austin." I gave him a little smile to reassure him. "I don't think this one is alien. His clothes seem to be from around these parts." I pointed at the shoes.

"Unless he stole those," Austin said.

"Possible," I answered. "It doesn't matter really. It's still someone breaking and entering."

"But why?" Arizona asked. "Is there a reason for someone to enter your home? He doesn't appear homeless or desperate."

"There is something here he wants. We must determine what the commodity is," Regulus said.

Chapter Six

Goliath

After loading the man's body into the Jeep, Austin turned to me and frowned. "Using my vehicle to haul bodies is getting to be a habit. These dudes really need to get a car." He looked from the two motorcycles sitting in my driveway to me and shook his head in disgust. "Is he out for much longer?"

"No, I saw him moving. What's the plan?" I wondered if there was one.

"We take him to the woods for questioning," Regulus answered without enthusiasm.

"Why not question him here?" I didn't know if I should ask or not. Regulus had a reason or he wouldn't go to the trouble.

As if reading my mind, Regulus said, "If this man is from another world, then we must take him to the

Vault for interrogation. If this man is from this world, then we must decide if he goes to the Vault or to your jails."

"Ah." I pretended to understand, but I still didn't know why we were going to the woods.

Austin grinned at me, evidently not fooled. "Yeah. I'm just along for the ride while the *Mission Impossible* guys do their thing. At least that's what I keep telling myself."

I returned Austin's smile until I saw the murderous look on Regulus's face. When Austin saw the expression, he winked at me. I frowned to discourage him. Touching Regulus's arm, I smiled, and he appeared to relax.

"Let's do this thing." I added some enthusiasm, hoping he'd stop scowling, and went to Regulus's motorcycle to wait for him.

Austin drove the Jeep with Arizona and we followed, my arms wound tightly around Regulus's waist. The wind chilled me, and I jealously thought of the heater inside the Jeep. I could see Arizona sitting shotgun in the Jeep, periodically turning his head to make sure we were still behind them. I snuggled in close to Regulus and burrowed my head in the hollow between his shoulders. His warm body shielded me from most of the wind.

The Jeep left the dirt road, and we continued to follow through the woods until we stopped at a clearing. I looked around to see if anything looked familiar. How did Regulus and Arizona find these obscure places in the acres surrounding my home? Miffed, I realized they knew these woods better than I did, and I'd lived here all my life.

Arizona hopped out of the vehicle. Regulus and I dismounted to watch as Arizona pulled the man's body from the Jeep. To my surprise, the man stumbled to his feet. His hands had been bound with rope, and Arizona steadied him by holding his elbow. Austin did nothing to help.

"Let me do the talking. OK?" Regulus stood with his back to the Jeep. I noticed the furrow in his brow that meant he was serious. He took both my hands in his. "No arguments. It is important for me to lead this questioning."

With my hands warm in his, I didn't want to argue. "Sure. I'll try to keep my mouth shut."

"This man is dangerous. Do you understand? He broke into your home and would have sliced you open from belly to sternum. We must find out who sent him."

I got a visual reminiscent of dissecting the pig fetus in biology class and nodded hesitantly.

Regulus released my hands. He turned and grabbed the man by his upper arm. Striding through the brush, Regulus forced his silent captive to stumble behind.

Arizona kept up with Regulus while Austin and I hung back a good distance. Austin shoved his hands into his jeans pockets and whispered to me, "They're not going to kill the dude, are they? That's murder, Mia. It doesn't matter that he broke into your house."

"Of course not. Regulus wants to question him. That's all." I hoped that was all.

Austin stared at me.

"Do you think they're going to torture him and then do him execution-style?" I laughed nervously.

"You watch too many movies."

Shrugging, he appeared to relax. "Things are weird now, and I really don't know what to expect." He raked his hand though his heavy bangs that always covered one eye. "Be careful, OK? These guys are in this on an entirely different level from you."

"No, they're not. I'm in this up to my eyeballs. Strangers are breaking into my house. I don't think I can get much deeper."

"If they hurt this dude, you're as responsible. I can't be part of some crazy torture interrogation. They need to go to the police with this guy."

"Are you nuts? And we tell the police that some guy broke in my room, and we suspect it has something to do with IIA? Maybe he's in cahoots with the folks from another dimension?"

Regulus and Arizona had stopped walking and were tying the man to a tree. I sat on the ground and waited for them to finish.

The man stared at me for several minutes before speaking. "Girl, you have messed up." His heavy Southern drawl surprised me. "They would have let you look for that brother of yours, but they won't let you break rules. You and the boyfriend—"

Regulus pointed at the man. "Do you think I care about whether I follow the rules with you? I could make you disappear." He paced back and forth with his hands steepled together as if contemplating that very action. "That would make it easier for me."

"He knows about us." I whispered the words but Regulus heard. An involuntary shaking started at my knees and quivered up my body. I pushed my hands to the ground to steady them. I wanted to hear what he knew. Why he cared.

The man's black eyes pierced my confidence. I looked away. Regulus and Arizona had bound him in a seated position against the tree in such a way that he couldn't escape or even struggle. Nevertheless, his eyes didn't show fear.

Regulus squatted on his haunches in front of the man so he was at eye level. His voice held a menacing tone I had never heard before today. "You are nothing to us. And nothing to the people who sent you. When you disappear, no one will miss you."

Austin moved forward. "Reg—"

"You sit down."

Regulus and Austin glared at each other. The air thickened with tension. An orange cloud of frustration glowed around both of them.

I had to intervene. "Austin, please sit by me. Let's stay out of it."

"Come with me, Mia. You've got to see how crazy these guys are." Austin leaned over to grab for my hand.

"I can't, Austin. You know I can't."

He rose slowly, and his fingers brushed my shoulder. "And I can't be a part of this. The dude was wrong, yeah. I don't do well in confinement, and this is heavy." Austin shifted from one foot to the other nervously. "I have to leave."

I was startled when Regulus sat on the ground next to me. "Arizona and I will be back. Can you stay here and guard this man with Austin?"

"Where are you going?" I asked.

"Hey man, I said I was leaving. You can't leave Mia by herself with this dude."

"No, that's why you'll stay. I need to find out if this man is in our jurisdiction." Regulus stood.

"Damn," Austin muttered so only I could hear.

* * *

A pair of owls hooted back and forth. Other than nature's background noise, no other sounds interrupted the night's quiet. Austin sat in silence staring at our prisoner. I knelt next to him on the ground, periodically checking my watch. I clicked the flashlight off. The batteries would probably last, but I didn't want to risk not having it if we needed it.

"What's been going on with you?" I studied Austin's face and hoped to read it in the moonlight. He didn't answer.

"I haven't really talked to you in weeks." I hoped the statement didn't sound accusing. My schedule had been filled with school and Regulus, both activities not involving Austin.

He still didn't respond. His eyebrows lifted in unison with his shrug. "You haven't been...available," he muttered under his breath. He shook the strand of hair from his eyes and continued to stare at the man tied to the tree.

"You're right. Sorry." I picked at the torn fabric on the knee of my jeans. "It's my senior year. I have a lot going on."

"That's not what I'm talking about."

"And Regulus and Arizona have been training me. I have to be able to protect myself."

"That's working out, huh?"

I stayed quiet.

"They're going to get you killed. You're in over your head, Mia. You're just a kid."

"And what are you?"

"Barely more than a kid." Then he laughed. The sound was dark and full of remorse. "I understood why you were involved in the beginning. We all want to find your brother." He stopped and took a deep breath.

"Go on," I said.

"This isn't about your brother now. The IIA is using you and you have to admit to yourself that Regulus is too."

"That's not your business."

"I'm your best friend." He paused. "Or at least I used to be."

"You still are."

"Then listen to me. You should get out of this while you can."

"He's right." Our prisoner's gravelly voice startled me.

"I wasn't talking to you. Shut up," I said to the man. I turned my attention back to Austin. "And thanks for the advice, but I can take care of myself."

"I don't think you can."

I straightened my back and counted silently to ten before answering. "I think the real problem is that you don't like Regulus."

"Yeah. You're right. I could candy coat it and lie to you. He doesn't care about anything but himself. It's all about the IIA, Mia. It's not about you."

"You're acting like a jealous boyfriend. We're

friends. That's all." I looked away, not meeting his eyes.

He didn't respond. Instead, he rose and approached to the man tied to the tree. Squatting down to eye level with him, Austin said, "Why did you break into Mia's house? We might let you go if you tell us the truth."

"Hey, you can't tell him that," I said.

"Sure I can."

The man nodded his head like a fishing bobber trembling above the water's surface.

Clearly encouraged, Austin continued, "You know about Mia, and I think you can't be bad if you're warning her to get out of this mess she's in. Why did you break into her room?"

The man stared at Austin in silence.

"OK, the clock is ticking on this one. Tick. Tock. Tick. Too bad. I'm in a really bad mood so—"

"I was supposed to get her," the man said and looked at me.

"Get her? Kill her?" Rising, Austin shook his head from side to side. "Man, you shouldn't have said that."

"No," the man sputtered. "Not kill her. Take her to the transport. I'd be done, and she'd be someone else's problem."

"Transport? Where to?" I wiped my hands nervously on my jeans.

"How would I know?" our prisoner said.

The man seemed a little too happy to say that he was ignorant of the details. I noticed that Austin had taken his pocketknife from his front pocket.

"You're going to let him go because he told you

that?" My exasperation was clear.

"No. I'm going to tell you about a class I'm taking this semester." Austin grinned in a lopsided fashion.

"Now?" I couldn't understand Austin's sense of humor sometimes and this was one of those times.

"My class, The Struggle of the American Indian, had a very interesting discussion on the method for scalping a person." Austin took his pocketknife and waved in front of the man's eyes.

My stomach twisted as I held my breath. I could smell the sour fear that exploded from our prisoner, like rank trash that I sometimes forgot to take outside at home.

Austin turned to me again. He lifted the small knife and held it poised above the man's head. "See? The scalping doesn't require a large knife. Just a sharp one to cut in a circle around the perimeter of this dude's head. Then I get a good grip on the scalp and yank. Voilà! Scalped."

I could see the whites of the man's eyes in the moonlit night. His heavy breathing filled the air.

I found my voice. "Gross, Austin. Stop it."

Staring into the man's eyes, Austin placed the tip of the pocketknife on the man's forehead. "Regulus and Arizona will probably kill him when they get back anyway."

I had watched Austin field dress a deer once after shooting it and knew that he wasn't squeamish. He'd cut the man to scare him if nothing else.

"I said, stop." My voice sounded high-pitched. "You don't have to do this."

The man had taken his eyes off Austin and watched me. I'm sure my anxiety came through loud and clear.

"Somewhere in Goliath," the man whispered. "That's all I know. I swear."

"Goliath?" Austin and I said in unison.

"Goliath. Down in south Arkansas. You know, the place where the Goliath Lights are."

Austin pulled the knife away from the man's head and snapped the blade into the handle.

"You going to let me to go now?" the man asked.

"Nah. You still broke into Mia's house. But thanks for the info." Austin smiled. Then he turned his head toward me and swept his heavy bang out of his eyes. "We need to find out what's in Goliath. Sounds like a road trip to me."

* * *

The cell phone is my pocket vibrated, startling me out of the trancelike state I had adopted while waiting for Regulus and Arizona to return. I rubbed my eyes tiredly and wished for a large cappuccino. I removed the phone from my jacket pocket to see the caller ID on the display.

"Hi, Em. How did you know something was going on?"

The voice on the other end sounded tired and a little grumpy. "Austin sent me a text. My phone is set to sound on those, so it woke me."

"Sorry." I scanned the woods to see Austin pacing around the tree. "What did he text?" I asked.

"He wants me to research the town of Goliath.

Does he know what time it is?" She hesitated for a moment and then said, "What's he doing with you in the middle of the night?"

Em could ask that kind of question. She knew how I felt about Regulus.

"A guy broke into my house through my bedroom window."

"No! You at the police station or something?"

"I'm in the woods with Austin guarding the guy." I was sorry the minute I told her that part. Not because we didn't tell each other almost everything, but this would be a hard situation to explain. I tried to summarize and failed miserably when every detail lead to more explanation.

"Give me the phone, please." Austin held out his hand. He had most likely gotten tired of listening to me retell the events of the night.

Lacking the energy to argue, I rolled my eyes and handed him the phone. The wind blew through the trees, and I closed the gap in the front of my jacket. My teeth began to click together before I could stop them. I moved to sit near a bush that would shield me from the wind. I studied our prisoner, who hadn't moved since he had answered Austin's questions.

"Yeah, yeah. Can you look it up?" He paused and grimaced while holding the phone away from his ear for a moment. "Please?"

I smiled because I knew that Em was giving him heck for waking her. I also knew that she wished that she could be with us, which made her crankier. When you have a mom like Em's, you're lucky to leave the house in daylight hours. The house would have to be on fire to leave after 10:00 p.m.

Fifteen minutes later, Austin's cell phone sounded with the beat of some heavy metal song that I didn't recognize. Before Regulus had come along, my cell phone would mysteriously chime with new ringtones every few days. I never knew how Austin snuck them onto my phone, and although I acted irritated that he had done it, it always amused me.

"Yeah... Uh-huh." Austin turned his back to me, and I rose to get closer to the conversation. "What else?" he asked.

I tugged on the back of his leather jacket. "What's she saying?"

"Just a minute," Austin said into the phone. He punched at the display and held it off in front of his mouth this time. "Go ahead. You're on speaker."

"You there, Mia?"

"Hey Em. Sorry we woke you up."

"It's OK. Better to be woken up by Austin than by somebody crashing through my window."

I laughed. "It's about the same."

"Here's what I found on Goliath. It's a bump in the road down in south Arkansas. Small population. Why do you want to know about it?"

"The guy who broke into my house said he was supposed to take me there. Great to know he was going to drag me to a place even smaller than Whispering Woods."

"Weird. He was going to kidnap you?" Em didn't sound too surprised. My life had jumped to an entirely different level from what could be considered normal.

"I guess," I said. "That doesn't tell us a thing."

"Anything else, Em?" Austin sounded as perplexed

as I did.

"Let me go back to my search page." The click of keys sounded. "Wait a minute." Excitement came across the distance loud and clear. "Sorry, guys. I looked it up only on the maps section earlier. This is very weird."

"What?" Austin and I said in unison.

"There's a million results here on something called the Goliath Lights." More clicking.

"What is the light?" Austin asked.

"They're famous for it. Apparently there's even been TV shows filmed about it," Em muttered, then...more unintelligible mumbles as though she was reading.

"Can you read out loud, Em? I asked. "The suspense is killing me."

"A mysterious light with a legend. There's something about a murder, a man's head being cut off, and other theories. A light will appear over some railroad tracks and some say it's the worker who fell and was decapitated and is looking for his head and..." Em trailed off.

"And what?" Silence. I fidgeted. "Em, keep going. And what?"

"Some scientists think it's due to some quartz crystals. That's about it," she said.

"I think we need to go see what's in Goliath," Austin said.

Chapter Seven

Fight

The crunching of dry, fallen leaves alerted us to the arrival of Regulus and Arizona. Grabbing my phone and pressing the button to activate the screen, I realized that the guys had been absent for two hours. I knew from one trip with them into another dimension that it didn't necessarily mean that they had been there for the same amount of time. Still, waiting was not my strong suit, and I glared at both of them.

Austin ignored them and continued to stare at the man we had tied to the tree. Earlier, he had played games and texted on his cell phone for entertainment. Guarding a prisoner had turned out to be a very boring gig.

"You're back." I got to my feet, then brushed some leaves and damp debris from the back of my jeans. My mind briefly went to the need for some stain spray at home, and I scolded myself mentally for letting my mind wander. Surely agents didn't have to worry about laundry care, but neither did most teenagers.

"Yes, back in a meteorite moment, as they say," Arizona said with a pleasant smile.

"Nobody says that." Austin stood also as he commented in a deadpan tone. "Unless you are from a galaxy far, far away. Wait. That would be you, wouldn't it?" Placing his phone back in his pocket, he came toward us with his usual swagger. Austin's confidence coupled with his sense of humor usually drew people to him. It did the opposite in this case.

"What did you find out?" I asked, wanting to divert the conversation away from the tension brewing. I looked at Regulus.

"Nothing." His answer was quick and even.

I couldn't help but be suspicious, although the delivery was pretty much the standard from him. Austin nonchalantly hung an arm over my shoulder, a habit he'd developed over the past year. Before Regulus had come along, it had never been an issue.

"If you would like to keep that limb, I recommend that you make a decision to keep your body off her." Regulus stepped forward. I thought that his shoes might even be bumping Austin's.

Oops. I hadn't slipped away from Austin fast enough. "Hey, no harm done. He didn't mean anything by that." I laid my hand lightly on Regulus's chest.

"You don't seem to be worried about it when you leave her in the woods with me for two hours while you play super-agent man. I can't even tell that you guys are dating except for the fact that you are always hanging around and needing help with your IIA gig. You have no idea what we've been doing together while you were gone." Austin was taunting Regulus. First he couldn't get along with Arizona and now Regulus. I was tired of this.

"She's mine." Regulus said in almost a whisper. He pulled me to his side.

"Um, wait a minute. I don't belong to anybody. You're acting like a caveman," I turned to Austin. "And you. You're being a jerk." I tried to disengage myself from Regulus. He held tighter.

"Maybe I've decided that you like jerks. It seems to work for this guy." Although I didn't think it possible, Austin got closer to Regulus's face. "I guess it must be his pretty face because it's not his personality." He flicked a careless finger underneath Regulus's chin.

Regulus let go of me, and I lost my balance. Before I even knew what had happened, he was on top of Austin, and both were on the ground. They ignored me as Regulus began punching Austin in the face. Arizona grabbed Regulus's arm and tried to haul him off Austin.

I knelt to help break them apart. After I shoved myself between them, Regulus hit me on the arm. I cried out, and he finally stopped.

Austin was glaring at me. One eye was already starting to swell shut. Blood ran from the corner of his mouth and his nose.

Regulus extracted himself from the tangle and stood. Arizona offered a hand to help Austin, who got up on his own. Regulus turned his back on Austin, which was either stupid or arrogant in light of what had happened. I heard him taking deep breaths.

Austin wiped his mouth on his sleeve. Blood was smeared on his cheek. "I'm done here. Mia, let's go."

Astonished, I looked at his battered face. "Austin, you can't drive right now. You won't be able to see the road and you're hurt."

"You staying or coming with me?" Austin demanded.

"I'll drive him, Mia." Arizona went over to the man tied to the tree. We had all but forgotten about him. "I'll drop this guy off at the portal first since we've been instructed to bring him to the Vault." He began to unwind the rope.

The man was smiling. His lack of concern about being taken to the Vault worried me.

Regulus went to stand by his motorcycle. "I'll take you home."

"Thanks," I muttered awkwardly. My anger at both him and Austin had disappeared, replaced by a flood of relief at the thought of going home to bed.

Arizona led the intruder to the Jeep without any struggle or force. I watched the man disappear into the dark backseat.

"You get in and watch our prisoner in the back while I drive," Arizona told Austin. Austin grimaced but didn't argue as he got into the backseat of his own vehicle.

The moon shone through the treetops enough to silhouette the three in the Jeep. I couldn't see that Austin was looking at me, but I could feel it. The engine started, and I watched the Jeep lumber slowly away into the darkness.

I wrapped my arms around myself and waited for Regulus to mount the motorcycle. He handed me a helmet, and I put it on before seating myself onto the bike. I wound my hands around his waist. He grabbed both my hands and firmly placed them to encircle his body.

We didn't talk and began moving. I was getting better at riding with him, but by the time we arrived at my front porch, I was too exhausted to think about all the things I wanted to say to Regulus. Sleep would be the best thing for both of us.

"We need to talk," he said, dismounting and helping me off the bike.

"I know. But I'm too tired right now." I must have sounded sad, but I could barely hold my head up.

"The man. He wanted something from you, and I have to figure it out. That is the reason I lost control. I'm sorry."

"Austin means a lot to me. You have to respect that. And I know that he was trying to get your goat."

"Goat?"

"Make you angry." I smiled at him. Sometimes it was easy to forget that he didn't know all the idioms.

"Yes, he got my goat."

I smiled even bigger. "We need to talk about us and talk about what the man told me and Austin."

Regulus set his hands on my shoulders. He squeezed gently and then his fingertips moved across my collarbone and up the sides of my neck in a quick caress of silent apology.

"What did he say?" he asked.

He stood quite a bit taller than me and I tilted my head to meet his eyes. "Something about taking me to Goliath," I said. At his quizzical face, I added, "A place down south a few hundred miles."

"How did you learn this?" He seemed so amazed that I had to laugh.

"Austin asked him. And not in a subtle way." I took the doorknob. "Can this wait until tomorrow?"

"Want me to come in?" Hands still on my shoulders, he bent his head.

"You can check the place out and that's it. Then you have to leave."

"Yes. Those are my intentions."

"I mean it. My dad has laid down the law, and you can't be in the house while he's gone." I made a point of sounding serious.

"I agree." He kissed me lightly on the forehead, not on the lips as I'd anticipated, then opened the door. "Let me check that it is safe before I leave."

Inside the house, "checking" included every closed door and possible hiding place. I followed him while stifling a half-dozen yawns. He held my hand some of the time, which was comforting. As much as I wanted to be upset with him over the fight earlier, I couldn't hold it against him.

Regulus took one look at my broken bedroom window and said he would call for a repairman the next day. We went to the garage and found some thin plywood to cover the opening. We couldn't tape it— the piece was a little large—so we propped it over the window. Then he pushed my tall chest of drawers in front of it.

"Everything appears secure. I would feel better if I slept on your sofa tonight," he said.

"Definitely not." I imagined myself trying to go to

sleep with him downstairs. And then I imagined my morning routine of flying around the house at warp speed to get ready for school. "No. I'll sleep with my cell phone in my hand if it makes you feel better."

"I'll call you in the morning before school," he said.

We went outside onto the front porch. The long porch swing at the end creaked in the wind. Winter was fast approaching, and I shivered again.

"OK. Don't you have late classes in the morning?" I envied Regulus's college class schedule. He didn't even get up until I was in second or even third period.

"Yes, but I'll still call. Maybe we can talk about what the man said about Goliath."

"There's not anything else to tell. Honest."

"I'll still call in the morning." He brushed his hand over the side of my hair and tucked a stray piece behind my ear. "When I tell you that Austin makes me... He makes me crazy. That's what you would call it. Then, do you think I am less than in control of myself?"

"No." I shook my head with more force than he probably expected. "Austin drives me crazy sometimes, but he means well."

"He means well with you. But he wishes me dead."

"That's not true. He doesn't understand you. It frustrates him." My argument sounded weak.

"Go inside and sleep." Regulus opened the door where I would go through. "And Mia."

"Yes?"

"I do not understand the myriad of thoughts in my head when I am with you." He rubbed his hand along the back of his neck.

"And I have no clue what that means. Myriad of

thoughts?" I wondered if he realized that people my age didn't use those terms. His training in the IIA obviously lacked a class in idiom usage and American slang.

Regulus stood silent and looked around my front porch for the answers. His eyes darted from the porch swing to the porch light and back again. "You know how you tell me that your words on a page are never in black and white but in a multitude of colors? And that the colors make it difficult for you to focus?"

I nodded. That illustration greatly simplified my condition, but the degree of my sensory awareness didn't matter. I got the point.

"Thinking about you is like that. My focus is pushed away by your smell and touch." He hesitated for a moment before continuing. "I should wait and talk with you tomorrow night instead of calling. I'll practice my patience."

"Practice away. It can wait."

Chapter Eight

Austin

Austin's character lumbered across the screen. Next, he climbed unsteadily since finding footholds in the game environment—the side of a cliff—wasn't an easy task. Austin moved his character's arm to swing his leather satchel over to one side of his body to maintain balance while leaning forward. Although it was a virtual world, physics still applied.

He peered to the right, then hefted his weight up and caught his foot in a crack of the stone. He launched himself up and lay atop the ledge. It was quiet. When he played online, he forgot about the noises of his room at home. The headset ensured that he heard the sounds of the virtual world of Zion and nothing else. Bird calls and wind rush filled his ears.

"It's about time," the voice said.

Austin's character jolted into an upright position.

"Hey man. Could you scuffle your shoes on the ground next time? Give me a little warning?"

"You were looking for me, right?" Pete answered.

"Yeah. Of course I was. Did you ever see me climb these eagle roosts for nothing?"

Pete laughed. "You're pretty lazy dude. You'll take on a fight if you have to, but other than that...no, you don't expend your life force."

Austin tapped his own forehead. "It's called smarts. Some people have 'em, some don't. Expend energy on the important things. Like finding you."

"What made you think you would find me on a mountaintop?"

"You're here, aren't you?" Although Austin's character didn't shrug, he lifted his shoulders nonchalantly. "I knew you were waiting to catch me again."

Pete's character, wearing a jumpsuit, sat down on the cliff's hard, slate surface. His feet hung precariously off the edge as if the drop were no more than a few inches. "How's my sis?"

Austin scooted beside him at the edge of the cliff. His feet swung back and forth. "She's better these days."

"Better how?"

"Not as gloomy and moody. Man, there's nothing moodier than a teenage girl, and she's been the worst. Now that she hopes she'll find you, and she's got her stud muffin hanging around, she's better." Austin began picking up small pebbles and tossing them over the cliff to watch them fall endlessly.

"She's not going to find me. Mia should get that idea out of her head."

"I found you." Austin's character waved his arm awkwardly toward Pete. "Here. Now I've got to figure out what you're running from."

"Running? I'm not running anymore. I just made a decision where there's no turning back. My life as big brother to Mia is over. No hanging out with the crew in Whispering Woods. No college." He paused. "No seeing my dad ever again."

"OK, man. Hold up 'cause you are a real downer. I climb this Herculean mountain and very nearly expend all my life force for you to tell me that it's game over? No one gets to pull you out of this deep cover gig you've got going?"

"The IIA wants me."

Silence filled the space. Austin couldn't hear a thing except for his own breathing. The living, breathing Austin squirmed in his chair while the character sporting a halo of golden dreadlocks sat still.

"It's going to kill Mia. She's agreed to help those dudes. She calls herself a team member." Austin hesitated, searching for the right term. "She's a portal tuner, locator, something."

"She's fine where she is."

"What? If the IIA is fine, why are they looking for you?"

"Mia has to make up her own mind. I made a decision for my life. I told you that I won't see my dad, my friends, anybody ever again. My regular life as a citizen is over." Pete's character stood.

"What's your hurry? I have more questions." Austin's character rose to face his friend.

"I can't stay any longer. Listen carefully. Look into

what is happening in Goliath. I'm on it, too, but she can read people and situations better than I can. Be smart. Use a cover when you go there. There's a ghost-hunting organization doing a trip this weekend. They'll let you sign up. It's safer to go with them."

"You don't care if the IIA knows about what Mia is doing? She'll tell her boyfriend. She's about disclosure these days," Austin said.

"Today, the IIA is the lesser of two evils. Tomorrow there might be three. Better that she's with them for now."

"And what if they find you?"

"Nah. The US government won't let that happen. And one more thing. My mom works for Bleeker. Sis needs to be aware of this. Whatever happens, Mia shouldn't trust her." Pete turned and jumped from the cliff in a graceful dive as if an ocean beneath would catch him. He accelerated to an alarming speed. After a burst of color, fabric expanded between his spread legs and arms.

He flew, and Austin watched Pete soar away.

Chapter Nine

School

Mr. Joseph paced the front of the computer lab, and then circled the perimeter of the room. I felt his presence as he stood behind me to inspect the work I might or might not have accomplished in the last thirty minutes. My eyelids felt like tiny lead weights pulled them down every time I exhaled.

"Miss Taylor? Are you having problems?"

"No, sir."

"You seem to be having a difficult time concentrating." He squatted beside my chair while holding the seatback with one hand. "You're behind on this exercise," he murmured. "It should take ten minutes to complete each lesson in the module. I don't believe in rushing people, but you normally finish before most."

"I didn't get much sleep last night. You're right, sir."

"I realize that your senior year is exciting, and students are easily distracted. Would you agree?"

That was a little like calling Hurricane Katrina a gentle breeze. "Um, yes."

"If you want to be successful in college, I suggest that you practice staying awake in my class and sleeping at night."

"Yes, sir." I kept my eyes on the screen in front of me.

"Why don't you come in after school and finish this exercise tomorrow? I'll let you catch up after you get some sleep tonight."

I frowned. I didn't trust teachers. Last month, my former science project mentor had turned into, uh, a huge disappointment. Dr. Eli Bleeker had fooled me and then ended up being psycho-killer teacher of the year. I wasn't falling for anything again.

"I could catch up in my study hall hour if you'll write a pass." I attempted a smile. My tired body and dry mouth protested. The fact that beauty queens used Vaseline on their teeth as an aid for constant smiling flittered across my delirious mind.

He wasn't smiling back. "I'll write a pass and expect you to finish the assignment."

"Definitely." I waited for him to leave while his loud breaths whistled through his nose. He was close enough for me to notice the gray hair in his thick mustache.

Because I'd twisted to talk to the teacher, I could see the class clown Tracy now holding up a piece of paper behind Mr. Joseph's back. I moved my head to better read it when Tracy yanked the paper back to his lap.

Mr. Joseph never turned. "Mr. Dorchester, you may bring me your amusing yet inappropriate illustration."

I might be a synesthete, but all teachers and parents obviously had a sixth sense.

A slight tittering flowed around the room before Tracy produced the paper. A tall boy with an artistic flair, Tracy had drawn Mr. Joseph with woolly eyebrows and an exaggerated smile. Beside him in the picture was a girl in jeans, her T-shirt stretched tightly over two large mounds. I don't know which was more embarrassing, the fact that he had drawn my breasts so big or that Mr. Joseph stood with his arm around me in a too-friendly way.

I cut Tracy a glare. *You'll pay later.* Slouching and self-conscious, I turned back to my computer screen.

The bell buzzed, and Mr. Joseph handed me the slip to come back during study hall. I pushed out of my chair and made a beeline for the door.

* * *

When I returned to the computer lab, Em sat alone in a corner of the room. Mr. Joseph nodded his head without looking me in the eye. Happy to be saved from my earlier embarrassment, I took the chair next to Em.

I started the module in my assignment for American government without enthusiasm. After finishing two modules in fifteen minutes, I leaned over to see Em's screen. The brainiac had obviously completed her assignments and was doing independent research on the Internet.

"What r u lookn 4?" I scribbled on a piece of scrap paper and shoved it at her.

"Anomalies in different counties in Arkansas. Sightings. Weird things." She wrote the words precisely in her neat cursive.

"Why?" I whispered, squirming. There had to be a good reason for this, and I was sure that I wouldn't like it.

"Just interested." She kept typing while she talked.

"Liar."

Em stopped to think for a moment before answering. "Tiny has a theory."

I stared at her. "You talk to Tiny?" Tiny didn't go to school and was older. He had the social skills of a Brillo pad—abrasive. I tried to imagine the two of them talking.

"Austin gave me his e-mail. He said Tiny was onto something but needed to know answers about you."

"Why didn't he e-mail me then?"

"You've been busy lately."

"Oh." What she didn't say is that I'd been spending time with Regulus. I guess Austin wasn't the only person I'd ignored lately.

"Miss Taylor?" I jumped at hearing Mr. Joseph's voice. I had completed my assignments, but I didn't want to leave. Em was up to something.

I focused on my screen until Mr. Joseph returned his attention to his newspaper. I wrote a note asking her to meet me after school in the parking lot. After letting Mr. Joseph know I had completed my work, I returned to study hall.

* * *

After school, the parking lot roared to life along with car engines. Everyone was escaping, as though they'd be locked in for the night if they lingered.

I spotted Em across two lanes of traffic, leaning on the side of Austin's Jeep while fastening her designer floral backpack. Its matching purse cost more than half my closet put together. She talked on her bling-covered cell phone and snapped it shut as I neared.

"We're going with Austin," she said.

I stepped over a water puddle in a low spot in the asphalt. Almost everyone had left the lot by this point, and Austin wasn't at the Jeep. Since Austin had graduated last year, I wasn't even sure why he was on school grounds.

"Where is he?" I yawned and covered my mouth.

"He'll be here in a minute. Think you can stay awake? Or am I boring you?" she muttered, clearly exasperated.

"Jeez, Em. I'm a little tired. Think you can give me a break?"

"Sure. Sure." She laughed. "You're cranky too. But," she said, holding up her hand. "It's understandable."

"Where are we going with Austin?"

"You'll see."

"I need to hear. Tell me now."

"Cranky to the max." She shook her head in

disgust. "Don't you trust me that this is important?"

"Sorry. Again." I thought about Regulus saying that he needed to practice patience. I could use some practice myself.

"Hello, my lovelies." Austin hung out of the passenger window of a pickup truck. It was covered in mud from the top of the cab to the bottom step rails.

"Hey." I shrugged the backpack off my shoulder and eyed the driver. I didn't recognize him. When I stepped closer, I noticed Austin's purple eyelid and bloodshot eye. I cringed.

"You had better hurry before she changes her mind and goes home," Em said to Austin.

"Joe was showing me a shortcut to Tiny's." Austin grabbed the bill of his baseball cap. "You ladies ready to rock and roll?"

Em and I nodded. Austin jumped out of the truck without even looking back at his friend. The truck sped off without a word from the driver. Taillights flashed as it braked hard at the cars lined up at the exit.

I jumped in the back of Austin's Jeep so Em could ride shotgun. She examined the interior of the Jeep, littered with empty soda bottles and snack wrappers on the console and floorboard. She lifted a brow.

Austin turned on music with a heavy bass beat, and the speaker in the back near deafened me. I tapped him on the shoulder and put my hands over my ears. He smiled and turned it up. Em reached over and turned it down.

"I thought you liked my music," he said.

"When I can hear it, yes. When the pounding turns

my cerebral cortex to mush, not so much," I yelled into his ear.

He turned the sound off. Silence. "If we don't have music, we talk. OK? Let's discuss how Regulus is stringing you along so you can do some of your portal finding if he needs it." He glanced at me in the rear view mirror and then back at the road.

"You have no right to say that. You don't know him." My guilt over Austin's bruised eye disappeared.

Em rifled through her purse as if she couldn't hear us. She produced a pack of gum, and I held my hand palm up between the front seats. Dropping a piece into my hand, she glanced at me while attempting a small, reassuring smile.

"I think he cares about her." Em pushed her bag to the side. "He's different from us, that's all."

"Different in that we're regular people not trying pretend where saving the world."

"It's not pretend. I don't know what your problem is. I'm friends with you. I'm dating Regulus. Do you see me asking you two to be best buds? No, I'm not. You should deal with it if you're my friend." I heard screaming, and it was me.

Em's eyes widened. "Mia, listen. Calm down. We don't want to see you get hurt. Your family went through so much when Pete disappeared and—"

"We? Oh, now you're on his side?" Had they had talked about this? Conspired to do an intervention? My chest ached.

Minutes later, the Jeep's tires sluiced through the mud and flung globules onto the windshield and windows. The hard rain earlier in the day had turned areas of the field into a brown and green mush. The four-wheel drive easily navigated through the mud, and Austin purposely cut corners to sling even more mud than necessary onto the windows.

He cranked up the music. Em put one hand on the dash and the other on a handle above her head to brace her body. I looked around for something hold on to. My hair whipped into my eyes at a violent turn that had Austin whooping in glee and Em yelling for him to slow down.

He continued through two more fields with some heavily forested areas between. I began to wonder when the wild ride would end when the back of a structure came into view. The small white house stood near a gravel road that we hadn't taken. He parked at the side, or what might have been a side, if the house had been square or even rectangular in shape. Instead the house looked as though various rooms had been added over the years whenever needed. Two speckled brown hound dogs waited for us to step out.

"They're friendly," Austin told us.

"Why didn't we take the road?" I exited the Jeep while grinning at Em. She stood balanced in a spot of drier ground, eying an enormous puddle of water between her and the house.

"Shortcut." Austin stomped randomly but missed the mud. He rapped on the wood frame of the screen door.

"Come in," a muffled voice shouted.

Austin opened the door, Em and I at his heels. The kitchen was small, and we passed in five steps through a doorway into the next room, where Tiny's voice filled the space. I looked from Tiny to the static ceiling fan that hung right beside his head from the family room's low ceiling.

"What's up, man," Austin said.

"Hi, Tiny," Em and I said simultaneously.

"Took you long enough to get here." Tiny turned his back and walked through another doorway. We followed while I looked at Em with my eyebrows raised. She ignored the silent question.

The room we entered was large, housing a long, high table along the length of one wall. I guessed it had been custom-built and served as a desk, the height accommodating Tiny's frame. Electronics lined every square inch of wall. Without windows, the room was lit by a hurricane lamp casting a glow in the corner.

"Hey, Tiny?" Em asked. "Mia has no idea why we brought her here. Take it slow, OK?"

"Can do, Em. But you really should have told her before now."

"I know." Em shrugged.

Tiny's voice had taken on a different quality when he answered her. He spoke with a courteous tone, full of respect. But Em and Tiny hadn't known each other a month ago. Something had been going on, and I felt like the outsider. I'd never considered that others might be keeping secrets.

"Are you guys going to tell me what's going on?" I stared hard at Austin, noting no guilt on his face.

"The rain messes with the satellite, so my internet connection flaked out earlier. I think it's fine now." Tiny sat in a chair and motioned for us to find a seat. Austin and Em found a couple of folding chairs and pulled them closer. "Sit," Tiny told me, voice irritated.

I obeyed, sitting on a nearby blue milk crate. I wrapped my arms around my knees and waited.

"Tiny got curious after another video of GameCon surfaced." Em sat back in her chair with an ease that showed me she'd been in the room before. "He decided to poke around and find out who posted it. Guess what?"

Silence. I realized that I needed to breathe before I passed out. Inhaling and then exhaling deeply, I said, "I give."

"Wrong answer." Austin grinned mischievously. "Try again."

"Guys, I'm tired and ready to go home. These games are getting old." I started to rise.

Austin motioned for me to sit. "The video was posted by a user with only initials for the username. It was posted by PA." He lifted his eyebrows.

"Uh, so?" I shrugged.

"PA stands for Peter Antares." Em said the words slowly to emphasize the enormity of the find.

"That's a stretch," I said in a mocking tone.

"What is it with you? Now that you have your boyfriend and your new IIA gig, you're not interested in finding Pete?" Austin accused me with each word. He stood, and the chair fell back. He bent and grabbed it without giving me any eye contact.

"That is not fair."

No one spoke for several minutes and Tiny, who had ignored the exchange, began typing on his keyboard, the words huge on his oversized monitor, so big I could see it from across the room.

"You both are immature," Tiny said so matter-of-factly that I felt my cheeks redden. "Listen up."

"Sorry," Austin said, still without facing me. He shrugged out of his jacket and tossed it to the side. "We're good. Show her, Tiny."

Tiny removed his toboggan cap, ran his fingers through his hair, and replaced the black knit hat. His red curls peeked out from the edges. He glanced over at Em. They exchanged loaded looks that unnerved me. Then his large hands moved in a flurry of key pounding.

A video came up on the monitor, its footage dark and grainy. I squinted and leaned forward until my elbow rested on my knees. There was no sound until a voice began to narrate.

"What is this?" I cleared my throat and shifted uncomfortably.

"Some footage from a new show about recent sightings of unexplained phenomena. It was on Tales of the Awesome and Eerie," Em answered. "It's some footage from Goliath."

"Oh." I wasn't sure if that explained anything.

The voice narrating pointed out a glow of light on the screen. The light was dim and didn't illuminate much as it bobbed over some railroad tracks. The narrator explained the theories surrounding the light and the legends that townspeople had handed down through the generations.

A reporter appeared in the camera view. "Scientists who study the phenomenon tell us that there is no clear explanation for the appearance of the light. Let's see what the citizens of this small town have to say about it."

The reporter then moved from person to person

allowing each to give a theory about the light.

"I think it's the railroad worker lookin' for his head. It got chopped off," said a little boy wearing a T-shirt with a tractor on the front.

"It's electricity given off by quartz," said a man standing beside the boy. "That's all it is."

At the end of the video segment, all three of my friends turned to me in unison and looked at me expectantly. I stared back, uncertain, and stood while chewing the edge of my nonexistent thumbnail. They all began to talk at once.

I held up my hand. "What's with the clip? I can see I missed something," I said.

"Think of this as an exercise in finding Waldo," Austin said.

Tiny turned back to the mouse and clicked to start the clip again. His deep rumbly voice narrated as he periodically stopped the footage to make sure I didn't miss anything.

"Don't watch the kid. Look at this crowd in the background. Here we have this black pickup truck with the spotlight mounted on the top. These dudes are talking with their backs to the camera. Got the camo gear on so they look like every other hunter wandering around town. This one on the right turns sideways and...now look at him." Tiny stopped the video.

I moved closer. "Oh. Nuh-uh. It can't be," I said.

But it was, or *he* was. Pete looked taller. His shoulders looked broader, and he'd gained weight.

Now I stood directly in front of the monitor, fixated. "He posted this video?" I asked.

"No," Em answered. "We never said that. He didn't

post this. We were looking for a clue about Goliath. We wanted to know if there would be some reason that the guy who broke into your house would take you there."

"Pete's in Goliath. He's been there this whole time? Is that what you think?" I paced in the narrow space along the wall. Each step came faster than the last.

Austin threw out an arm to stop me. "He's there for a reason. No, we don't think he decided to move to Goliath. This mysterious light and Pete are connected somehow. And you. We need to figure out what's going on." He squeezed my hand.

"I know that." I looked at Em and Tiny. "You guys need to stop keeping things from me."

"You kept secrets from us too," she said. Em's voice held no recrimination. Today she wore a flannel shirt over a black T-shirt. The combination might have been a standard in my closet but not in Em's. Her hair was held back in a ponytail, another uncharacteristic style choice for her. "At first, you didn't tell us about your synesthesia, about meeting Regulus and Arizona—"

"Yes," I answered. "You're right. I was scared you'd think I was a freak. I needed you." I broke eye contact with her. "Things are different now."

"True," Austin said. He picked up a yellow stress ball with a smiley face from the floor and threw it from hand to hand as he talked. "The way I see it, we're now a team of superheroes. You know, fighting to save the world from ultimate doom. But without the leotard outfits."

I grinned. Austin always made me smile, and I hadn't let myself go with him for a long time.

Em walked over and grabbed the stress ball in midair. "And we have a little more brain than brawn."

"And only one of us has superpowers," Tiny said.

Em looked at Tiny, smiling. "Tiny's written some code that puts a cookie on any computer that visits his website. At GameCon, he thought that turnabout is fair play. If someone put a tail on him online, then why couldn't we do the same?"

I nodded and attempted not to look too amazed at all they had done while I wasn't paying attention. "Did anything turn up?"

"Yeah. I detect several IP addresses that are watching my activity. I don't like people in my business, but I hope they keep hanging around. I have something special planned to blow their minds." Tiny chuckled, sounding devious.

"Tiny is doing what he does best. In the meantime, we've contacted a ghost hunting team and we'll meet them in Goliath this weekend. We don't think Regulus and Arizona should be there. If Pete is around, he won't come forward if they're with us." Emily threw the stress ball in my direction.

I grabbed the yellow, squishy ball. "Pete was obviously trying to warn me against Dr. Bleeker when he's left messages in the past. Why can't Regulus and Arizona go with us? What in the heck does a ghost hunting team have to do with this?" I stopped the rush of questions to take a breath and sat on the edge of a wooden table to stop myself from pacing.

"This is a coming clean meeting. I have something else to tell you." Austin rarely sounded so serious. His dark hair hung over his eyes like a shield while he focused on his knees. "Pete's contacted me and Tiny."

"What?" I managed the words in a barely a whisper. I looked at Em and she looked back with no apology.

"On *Quest*. We've run into him a couple of times online." Austin finally peered at me between strands of hair hanging over his eyes.

"When? How many times and what did he say?" I didn't have time to get mad or let my feelings get in the way. I made the decision to suck it up.

Austin sat back and relaxed at my calm tone. "Two times," he said. "Both were very brief. No hanging around and shooting the breeze. He mainly wanted to either ask a question or tell us something."

"He sent you a chat message in *Quest* two times?"

"That's not what I said. He didn't chat. He showed up. Playing the game."

"Using his old character?" I couldn't imagine that he would do that since he had been in serious hiding all this time.

"Of course not," Tiny said. "But it was him. Came right up and joined us while playing."

"How do you know it was him?" I hated to sound skeptical, but I had learned some lessons in trusting people. Just because something walked like a duck and quacked like a duck, it didn't mean it was a duck. Maybe it had feathers and a beak, but...

"We know in the same way that you would know. You can't fake some things. It's Pete."

"Back to the questions. Let's assume it's him. What did you find out?" I asked.

"Number one is that Pete asked me and Tiny to

look out for you. Like you're in some kind of danger," Austin said. "Number two, he doesn't trust your boyfriend and his devoted sidekick."

"I think he doesn't know Regulus and Arizona so he's not trusting anyone outside our circle," Emily said quickly with a smile. "Don't let Austin make you think you have to choose between your boyfriend and your brother. They're not on opposite sides."

"OK," I said. I appreciated Em's effort to keep the conversation civil and fair. "I'm going to tell Regulus and Arizona about what you're telling me today. It's not because Regulus is my boyfriend. It's because I can't live with secrets and not trusting everybody. I trust them even if you don't." I looked pointedly at Austin and Tiny.

"Sure. I knew you would. It took this long for us to decide that it all has to be out in the open between us." Austin leaned back. "Another question?"

"Number three?" I asked.

"The Goliath connection is important," Austin said.

"I had that feeling already. What's with the ghost hunting? You think there are ghosts there?"

"No. Pete advised that we hook up with them because there's safety in numbers."

"I don't understand."

"Nothing will happen to us when we're there because we'll be part of a documented group that caters to strangers in town."

"That's sort of brilliant," I said. "It's like a cover."

"And there's some crazy stuff going on in that town, and they have nifty equipment," Austin said. "One thing you have to agree to."

"Shoot," I said.

"Leave Regulus and Arizona out of the trip. Tiny won't go either. Just you, me, and Em."

I stared at him for a moment before letting myself look over at Em and Tiny. Their faces were expectant. They had already discussed this.

"OK."

"Oh, there's one more little thing Pete said the last time." Austin looked uncomfortable.

"What?"

"Your mother works for Bleeker, and you shouldn't trust her. Ever."

"No news to me. Same relationship I've always had with her." I hesitated and then added, "Correction. We don't have a relationship, Austin. Thanks for the tip."

Chapter Ten

Doubts

The sound of a sports announcer on the downstairs television told me that Dad was probably napping in his recliner. He always said football games were the best for lulling him to sleep on a lazy Saturday afternoon.

"I think that you need to know more about the people coming through the portals," Em stated. "The corporation listed on the business card you think Pete left is legit. They're doing some good research."

"Uh-huh," I said with a certain amount of skepticism. She hadn't been with us last month when we'd found the dead bodies. Of course, I had told her everything. But hearing about an experience and actually being there are miles apart.

"Seriously. If I didn't know what I know—about Bleeker I mean—it would be hard to criticize the Aidos Company." Em lay back on my bedroom floor to join me as I reclined, staring at the ceiling. "They did find that injections of a certain mouse gene might cure diabetes in humans."

"Mice. So they have a legitimate front. He's still a murderer."

"I'm not saying that he's not. And I'm not sure you can link him to this company based on a hunch. I've looked at every reference that mentions the company. No Bleeker is ever listed as an employee or scientist working for them."

"I figured that. Bleeker's probably an alias. I don't know how to find out the real name. And then he might not be using his real name at Aidos."

"Tiny's been doing a lot. He knows that he can find out something if he can break into some national security information."

My jaw dropped. "No way," I said, shaking my head back and forth. "He cannot do that. Even if he could do it, he can't risk getting caught. That's like federal offense type stuff."

"I said the same thing to him," Em said.

We both lay looking at the ceiling in silence for a few moments. Biscuit sauntered over, plopped down next to me, and laid his chin on my arm. Comforted, I rubbed his head. "And he's doing something that could land him in federal prison."

She cleared her throat. "He said he's finding other ways. He says that he can eavesdrop on key players in government because they often use private e-mail addresses and websites to discuss stuff that people should only be discussing on a highly secured site. Tiny says he's less likely to get caught this way."

"He can get in less trouble."

"Maybe." She shifted and turned to lie with her arm thrown up above her head. "Listen."

"All ears."

"Couldn't you leave all this alone?" She hesitated for a moment and then continued. "I mean, if Bleeker would kill to test out his gene stuff, he'd kill you. Dead."

"I know." I tried to speak nonchalantly so she wouldn't think I was scared. My voice betrayed me by squeaking.

"You're not responsible for finding Dr. Bleeker. I've been thinking. We could leave and go to college out of state. You and Regulus could see each other. We could drive home most weekends. We could be roomies."

"I couldn't do that." I shook my head. "Why would I do that?"

"Because this is a dangerous situation. Pete disappeared, and we don't know how related that was." She started to pick at the carpet between us. "You're putting your dad in danger. Your friends in danger. Yourself."

Em knew I would do anything to protect my dad. It was unfair of her to bring him into this argument, and she knew that. That hadn't stopped her.

I took a deep breath. "You can stay out of it. I won't hold it against you. If you're scared of what's happening, I'll understand."

The silence sat thickly between us.

Em rolled to look up at the ceiling again. "You shouldn't say that. I'd never leave you in this alone. I wanted you to see that there are alternatives."

"I see that there are no choices, Em."

"Everybody has choices. The question is whether you will choose to see them or not."

* * *

"Hey, watch out." A slim man with a shiny head unloaded supplies and equipment from the back of his SUV. His mustard-colored turtleneck sweater made his neck seem long and narrow. I thought of a giraffe carrying boxes and suppressed a giggle.

Em and I scooted away a couple of feet to clear a path for unloading. Since they said we couldn't touch anything until they organized the equipment, we both stood awkwardly watching. Austin had disappeared in search of sodas after being told to wait.

We were a couple of miles from Goliath. Everyone's cars sat in a small circle of bare earth that served as a makeshift parking lot. Although we weren't far from the freeway, no other cars, not even one, rumbled along the dirt road. The dense foliage lining the nearby railroad track hid the outside world from view, giving us a view of only the metal rails and occasional discarded timbers.

I shoved my hands into my pockets and shivered. Goliath was *cold*. My hoodie was warm enough, but I wished that I'd worn gloves.

Em looked toasty in her wool sweater, gloves, scarf, toboggan cap, and boots, ready for a blizzard. "Here, take my scarf. I'm hot," she said.

I smiled. "You sure?"

"Yeah, yeah. My mom made me put all this on. It's not that cold out here."

"OK, then. Thanks." I reached for her pretty pink scarf. "How'd you get permission to stay out all night?"

"Said it was a school assignment. Sounded really legit."

"Smart."

"They're afraid I'll let my grades slip since it's our senior year. I could tie anything to a grade and they'd say yes. What about you? Your dad doesn't care?"

"Nah."

"Your dad traveling this month?"

"Not every day." We hesitated to talk about anything more personal as the crew worked around us, carrying bags to an area near the railroad tracks.

A brunette wearing a navy suit approached. I studied her polished looks and briefly felt envious of her and Em. The feeling quickly passed. At least Em was naturally pretty. This woman's makeup would take an hour at least.

"Hello, girls," the woman said, her teeth blinding.

"Hi," Em answered with a bright smile.

The brunette looked around, and then her gaze returned to us. "Busy around here this morning."

Em and I nodded awkwardly. I snuck a look at Em and raised my eyebrows. Shifting from foot to foot, I waited for the woman to say something.

"I'm Alexandria." The woman held out her hand. I zeroed in on her shiny silver rings and red nails.

Em took her hand. "Emily."

I wondered if the woman belonged with the crew. "Mia Taylor," I said, without taking her hand. I wasn't trying to be unfriendly, but wished she would clue me in. "Alex, are you with our group?" I asked.

"Alexandria." Her smile irritated me. "Yes, I'm here as an observer." She leaned forward and whispered, "I'm a reporter. They don't allow reporters to attend, so I'm here as a participant."

That was interesting. I wondered if they would throw her out if they knew. This group had been pretty no-nonsense, judging from the sign-up process. Alexandria's clothing should have been a clue that she didn't add up to the usual guest. Her kitten heels yelled "suspicious." Em was fashionable but prepared in her barely-worn suede boots. Alexandria was ready for a business meeting. Or a photo shoot. I toed the dirt with one sneaker.

Austin parked and hopped out of his Jeep. "Hello, ladies." He held three cans of soda.

"Thanks." Em took a can from Austin. "This is Alexandria. She's a guest. Like us."

Not like us. I pursed my lips and stopped before the words popped out of my mouth.

"I'm Austin." He smiled at her, then looked at me. "Here's yours."

I took the soda and glanced from Austin to Alexandria. I really wanted her to leave before she got too comfortable. She wasn't with us, and I wanted it to stay that way.

"Here, would you like a drink?" Austin held out the soda can to her. My mouth dropped open. He was offering her his soda and thus inviting her to be part of our group. I wanted desperately to stop him.

Alexandria smiled brilliantly. "Oh, I couldn't take the last one. Isn't this one yours?"

"I'm really not thirsty. I wanted to get a look at the place and that gave me an excuse." Austin practically shoved the can into her hand.

"That's what I needed," Alexandria said. "Thank you so much!" She gave him an even bigger smile, and I wondered how much dental work she had. All she needed to do now was start waving a stiff hand from a convertible while wearing a sash.

A package slid to my feet as a guy walked by me. I bent for it, and my head hit something hard. "Ouch!" I straightened, blinked, and laughed.

The guy facing me rubbed his forehead. "Sorry about that. I might have a concussion. What about you?"

"I'll live. Oh, here." I handed him the brown package. I examined the twentysomething guy and decided immediately that I liked him. He had an honest face and exuded a warm yellow aura. I smiled back.

"You guys are first timers, right?" The guy asked our little group.

"Yes," I answered. "It's that obvious?"

He chuckled. "Bob tends to make the new ones stand back and watch in awe of our scientific processes. I'm Cade, by the way."

Austin stepped forward a little. "I'm Austin. This is Mia, Em, and Alexandria," he said, nodding his head toward each of us.

Great. Beauty queen was now officially part of our group.

"Want to give me a hand?" Cade asked Austin.

I frowned at the sexism. "I will. Point to something, and I'll be happy to carry it."

"Sure. Follow me." Cade led the way to a van parked beside the SUV. I walked beside him with Em close behind. Austin and Alexandria brought up the rear.

Cade gestured inside the van. "There's a few more things to grab. We're going to set up a tent canopy as headquarters. We've got some chairs and a small card table to go underneath it. Put the canopy over there." He pointed.

After watching him walk away, I grabbed some chairs in nylon bags, finding them bulky rather than heavy. Em located another armful of chairs to carry. We lugged them toward the designated area. Austin lifted the folding table and tucked it under his arm. I glanced over my shoulder to see Alexandria standing with her arms folded, staring at the inside of the van. She shrugged and followed.

A smacking sound came from somewhere behind me, and I turned. Beauty Queen's heels had stuck in the mud. The sucking sound made me grin.

I stopped short of the area Cade had indicated, where he waited with an armload of stuff. "Austin, if you can set up that table, I'll put some of these electronics on top of it." Cade turned to me. "You can put those chairs anywhere. We can set that canopy up first."

Em and I followed orders and began the setup, removing chairs from the nylon bags and unfolding them into seats. Again, Alexandria stood watching, pouting a little.

"Is this what you do full-time? As a job, I mean?" I asked Cade.

"Hell, no. You don't think I get paid, do you?" He

laughed while assembling the telescoping rod that would be one corner of the canopy frame. "I work for the fire department here in Goliath. The rest of our team's from nearby towns. Nobody here does this for a living."

"Oh."

"It's a hobby...or obsession for us. We love it and would pay to do it. Actually, if you count the investment in equipment and travel expenses out of our pockets, most of us do pay."

"Why do you guys charge, then? For us, I mean." I didn't want to sound rude. The ticket price wasn't much. I didn't even have to ask my dad for the money but paid it out of my savings jar.

"We'd like to have some equipment in the future. A thermo-imaging camera would be nice." He hesitated and looked around for anyone who might be listening outside the five of us. "It's really a luxury we don't need. Totally unnecessary. Bob thinks we need it."

"You do this every weekend?" I asked him.

"Pretty much. Someday, I'll be married and have a family that will tie me up. For now, it gives me something to do that I'm interested in."

"You have a girlfriend?" Alexandria asked.

I thought the question was extremely rude since we had only met the guy. Em's eyes met mine and I guessed she felt the same. Beauty Queen must be interested.

"No," Cade answered nonchalantly.

"How can you expect to date if you're doing this every weekend?" Alexandria wanted to know.

I decided to save Cade some embarrassment. "The

chairs go under the canopy, right?"

Cade turned to me and smiled. "Yes," he said as he walked over to grab one nearby. With his back to Alexandria, he winked at me. "We need chairs in case people get tired."

While Em and I arranged chairs underneath the newly erected canopy, Austin helped Cade unpack a few electronic items on the table—a laptop, an audio recorder, a small, handheld video camera, and a digital thermometer.

One of the gadgets wasn't familiar. "What's that?" I asked.

"EMF meter."

"What do you do with it?" I picked up the small handheld that resembled a walkie-talkie.

"Detects fluctuations in electromagnetic fields." Cade picked up a notebook and pen. "Anybody here a good note taker?"

"Don't look at me." I nodded my head at Em. "She'd be great. She takes the best lecture notes of anybody at school."

"Em it is," Cade said as he handed Em the notebook. Em appeared so pleased at the assignment that I would swear she glowed.

"Why electromagnetic fields? What's that going to show us?" Austin asked.

Cade turned toward him. "Paranormal phenomena will have lots of EMF activity recorded in the area around them."

"What about me? What can I do?" I asked. I pushed up my sleeves to emphasize the fact that I was there to work. I stole a glance at Alexandria, who sat in a chair beside Austin. Her head was turned, and she wasn't listening but instead watched the other members of the team. The head guy, Bob, walked along the railroad track talking to a woman wearing a camo hunting jacket.

Cade picked up the video camera. "You know how to work one of these?"

"I bet I can figure it out." I took it from him and examined the buttons. The camera fit nicely in the palm of my hand with an LCD screen that flipped out to the side. "Battery life?" I asked.

"Four hours. But you can practice on it all you want. We have extra batteries that are charged and ready to replace," Cade said.

"We're going to be here all night, right?" I asked.

"Yes. Most paranormal activity takes place at nighttime, so that's when we're out here." Cade fished a bag from his backpack. He extracted a lighter and some mantles for the Coleman lantern that sat in the middle of the table.

Darkness fell early due to daylight savings time, but we completed unpacking and set up before night closed in.

"Dinner time." Cade walked off, and we looked at each other, unsure if we were to follow or wait. Eating hadn't occurred to me. I checked my watch and remembered that I'd promised to call Regulus. I drifted away from the canopy tent.

"Hey," I said into my cell phone.

"Hello. I'm glad you are calling. I was worried." The tone in Regulus's voice was clipped and unhappy.

"No need. You know I can take care of myself."

"Yes. I am completely aware of your fearlessness in the face of danger." He didn't make it sound like a compliment.

I smiled. "Ah, you miss me. And you want to be in charge of this mission we're on."

"I am obviously not in charge of what I should be. You were to text me. Team members should be in constant contact."

I imagined Regulus rubbing his wrist where the chip implant pebbled the skin imperceptibly. The chip guaranteed constant awareness of any team member. Regulus always knew Arizona's location.

The IIA had requested that Regulus take me back through the portal for my insertion procedure. The thought made me more than nauseous. It scared the daylights out of me, because nothing would ever be private again. My excuses to avoid the procedure were equally never ending.

"Sorry. We were helping to unpack and set up camp," I said sweetly.

Silence.

"Listen...I get it. You're worried sick. I'll be careful. We're checking the place out to see why somebody wanted to bring me here. We need to know why Pete's been here. It's important."

"Yes. I understand."

"What are you and Arizona doing tonight?" I asked, hoping to lead the conversation in a different direction.

"Arizona has requested that we attend a party. He says we appear strange and standoffish. This cannot be true. He mentioned that we must blend."

I laughed at the mental picture of Regulus

standing uncomfortably on the sidelines while Arizona flirted with as many girls as possible.

"I would be happy to go if you were there also," he said in a low, serious voice.

My mood changed. "It's only one night. I'll be back by dawn."

The phone clicked off. No good-bye or plans to see me in the morning. I blinked before walking back toward my friends. Austin stared at me with narrowed eyes while Beauty Queen talked to him. I ignored him.

Chapter Eleven

Ghost Hunt

After a dinner of cold sandwiches from the local sub shop, everyone discussed the goals for the night and the duties as assigned for each individual. Alexandria had somehow escaped an assignment except to observe all peculiarities and make sure Em logged them in the notebook.

The glimmer of the LED flashlight cast an unflattering glow over Alexandria's face, giving her a sallow look. Each time she began to ask questions, the woman I had dubbed Camo Lady would shine the flashlight in Alexandria's face. It was difficult not to giggle. Her need for attention was evident because she kept opening her mouth with useless questions. She never stopped, and Em recorded none of it. Even Em had grown tired of the incessant conversation. Austin seemed unbothered, which annoyed me more than anything else.

He'd been given the job of photographer, to take continuous photos even if nothing appeared to be going on at the site. I stood at a different angle with the video camera and did the same thing. I only had to keep my handheld pointed at Bob, Cade, Camo Lady, and a man named Ralph. Ralph carried an audio recorder in his hand and appeared to be extremely bored. He never said a word.

Bob and Camo Lady, on the other hand, talked non-stop. They talked to each other and to the camera. At one point, Cade flashed a smile at me, and I knew we must be thinking the same thing. How could you know if anything unusual was going on if you're talking the entire time?

After walking a half mile over rugged terrain and past a rotting train trestle, Bob held the EMF meter and talked while facing the camera. "This particular EMF meter is a trifield meter and will detect activity that emits electrostatic and ion energies. It will also detect magnetic energy. It is very sensitive. We can detect electromagnetic activity from wiring."

"Doesn't it find the ghosts for you?" Alexandria's voice grated on my nerves.

"No, it does not." Bob's tone reflected how I felt about her.

"Then why are you using it?" Alexandria asked. She stumbled and steadied herself using Austin's arm.

"Because a high EMF field can affect people adversely. It can cause paranoia and other psychological conditions. This may explain the reported instances as opposed to actual paranormal activity," Bob said, looking into my video camera. He continued to lead our group in a march past a second train trestle.

My personal radar had been going off the entire day, and I knew all too well what that meant.

After learning that I could find the portal no matter where it moved in my woods, I often tuned into background noise. Then, sensory perceptions I might have ignored in the past came forward, like Muzak in a department store. If I tried to listen, I could hear it or feel it. If I wanted to tune it out, I could shove it one layer down.

Now, I felt the buzzing and pulling that encircled a void of sound and light. The knowledge that a portal sat somewhere in the area made my stomach do somersaults.

Cade signaled me when we reached a third trestle, which seemed as worn as the other two. "Let's take a look around. We'll stay here for a while. Reports have occurred in different locations, but this is where most of the sightings have been."

Bob stumbled as he walked, not watching his path but looking at the EMF reader in his hand. "Yeah, I can definitely see the reading shows high amounts of electromagnetic activity in this very spot."

Cade tilted his head to look at the sky. "Power lines."

"Maybe," Bob turned to Em and began reciting numbers for her to record.

Camo Lady, whose real name escaped me, stood by and waved her flashlight around, lighting the camp. "Yeah, I need a break from walking. Be ready with the cameras, just in case."

I pressed the Pause button and lowered the

camera, which had become incredibly heavy after holding it at chest level for over an hour, the way my arm had felt after practicing knife throwing in the woods with Regulus. Maybe I did need to bulk up the arm muscles.

"This isn't what I expected. When is something going to happen?" Alexandria pouted and looked around as if she'd see a chair. She pulled her shoes off and bent to rub her feet.

"Are you new at this?" I asked.

She frowned. "I'm new...like you. You haven't ever been on a ghost tour either."

"Paranormal investigation," Cade said. "Not a ghost tour."

Austin sidled toward Alexandria. "I bet your feet hurt, don't they?" His voice was sympathetic and sweet.

I wanted to throw something at him. "No, that's not what I meant. New at her reporter gig."

Bob stiffened. "What do you mean, reporter?" His eyes darted from Alexandria to Camo Lady to me.

"It's not a big deal," Alexandria said. "There's no need for you to get upset."

"You misrepresented yourself," Camo Lady said.

"No one asked me what I do in my career," Alexandria smoothly stated. "It would be discrimination to let these kids do this and turn me away due to my profession."

"Kids?" I sat on the ground and placed the camera beside me. "At least we had the sense to wear the right shoes for an outdoor investigation." I stressed the word "investigation" and Bob smiled approvingly. I began tightening the laces on my sneakers.

"Hold up." Austin grinned at me. "She didn't mean anything by calling you a kid."

"I only meant that the three of you are young," Alexandria said. She had included Austin in her reference.

I smiled and knew I resembled a Cheshire cat. "Yes, Austin, we youngsters—"

"Shut your damn mouths." Camo Lady was gesturing wildly. "Look over there."

"Are you getting this? Get the camera." Bob's voice had lost its calm, documentary narrative tone. He couldn't take his eyes off a light dimly glowing in the distance. The circular object was whitish-blue and basketball-sized.

I retrieved the camera and frantically searched for the Record button. Em wrote notes while looking up at the light. Jumping to my feet, I glanced at Austin and saw him doing exactly nothing. "Psst. Austin, pictures," I said.

Austin lifted the camera and began shooting.

Alexandria squealed, the sound sending a shiver up my back and a metallic taste into the back of my mouth. I moved away from her.

"The object in question appears to be in the vicinity of the tenth mile marker along the highway, right over the railroad track. We'll move closer to see if we can determine more about the mysterious light." Bob had regained his composure and narrated clearly.

My stomach tightened in a knot, and the buzzing in my ears diverted my attention for a moment. I forced it away. Calm, I thought. As we walked, I chewed on my bottom lip. I knew this sensation.

Unless I had suddenly developed an awareness of ghosts, this feeling screamed "portal" to me. I couldn't stop walking, but I desperately needed Austin and Em to know the fact that had burst into my consciousness like a ray of sunlight through a cloud.

"The EMF meter is going crazy. Look at this reading." Bob then dictated numbers for Em to record in her notebook. "I've never seen this level of activity—"

A noisy motor speeding toward us interrupted Bob's speech. Everyone turned to look at the car pulling off the dirt road that ran parallel to the tracks. Its headlights blinded us until all I could see was a circle of light. We all held up hands and arms to shield our eyes.

"Stop. You are on private property." The authoritative command cut through the dark night.

"We have permission to be here." Cade spoke up first. His tone was friendly and noncombative. "Can you turn those lights off?"

A man in uniform approached us with a Mag flashlight. He flashed it in our eyes, which wasn't necessary since we were already blinded.

"I am Officer Sanchez. I need identification from everyone in this group." The man spoke with a slight accent.

"I don't have ID on me," I said with my hand shielding my eyes. I still couldn't see his face.

"That will be a problem," Officer Sanchez answered.

"You don't have a driver's license or ID? My instructions on the website strictly outline the necessity for these items on any paranormal investigation—"

"I didn't read all the instructions," I said sheepishly.

"Let me see the other identification cards." Officer Sanchez shone the flashlight at everyone's pockets.

Austin flipped out his wallet for the officer. "Here's mine."

Bob and Cade located their wallets. Camo Lady pulled out a man's wallet from her pocket.

"My purse is in Austin's Jeep," Em said. "I'll have to get my ID from there."

"Mine is in my car," Alexandria said.

"OK, let's go get those." Officer Sanchez led the way. "Is yours in your purse as well?" he asked me.

"Um. No. I didn't bring a purse." I started to sweat. I tried taking deep breaths while telling myself to stay calm. It wasn't as though I'd be thrown in jail or something.

"No purse? Where do you keep your lipstick?" Alexandria sounded shocked.

I looked at her like she was stupid. Very stupid.

"And your money?"

"My money is in my pocket. I didn't drive, so I didn't bring my driver's license." I ignored the lipstick question.

"I can vouch for her, Officer." Em smiled sweetly. Thank goodness for her.

"There have been several acts of vandalism in this area," Officer Sanchez stated. "I need to run all names to make sure that no one shows up in the system."

"OK. Maybe you can call my dad," I said.

"Let's take care of the others right now. Tell me your name and address." He took all the driver's licenses offered, jotted my information onto a small pad, and went to his vehicle. The sound of his voice over his radio cut through the quiet of our team standing in a circle.

When Officer Sanchez returned, he said, "All these IDs check out. Your group can walk back to the location of your vehicles. I'll need to see the other two IDs."

Our group walked parallel to the road while the officer drove his car to accompany us. No one said a word. At Austin's Jeep, Em retrieved her wallet from her purse and produced a license. Alexandria handed her license to Officer Sanchez. We watched the officer take both items to his car.

"This is crazy," I said to Austin. "Something's up. We weren't doing anything wrong."

"Shh," said Bob. His mouth puckered into a tiny point. "If you had read the guidelines for this excursion—"

Officer Sanchez returned and handed Em and Alexandria their cards. "We do have one problem," the officer said. He eyed me. Em was twisting a strand of hair nervously. Austin had a comical fake smile plastered on his face. Bob looked upset.

"I know. Did you call my dad? Maybe he can fax my ID to your station."

"You will need to come to the station with me," he said.

"What?" Austin, Cade, and I asked in unison.

"Am I under arrest?" The alarm must have been evident on my face.

Officer Sanchez shook his head that I wasn't. "Until I have some identification, I can't release you to continue with this group. The rest of you need to vacate this private property immediately."

"But I'm not under arrest, right?" I planned to find this out.

"I'm calling your dad. He can't take you to the station for not having identification." Em turned to the officer. "We know our rights. We watch television, you know."

"I'm glad you have studied the law on TV." Officer Sanchez smiled with phony warmth. "I am still asking you to accompany me to the station."

"Why?" I asked.

Officer Sanchez looked startled at my question. "Miss, I can arrest you for trespassing, or you can go with me willingly."

"You can't arrest me." I blurted the words before thinking and backed up.

Officer Sanchez grabbed my arm to stop me. At the same moment, my foot lodged into a hole in the grassy field. I fell backward, taking him with me.

I yelled out of surprise more than anything. The officer's knee came down hard on my thigh and pinned me to the ground. The falling Maglight beamed across his startled face momentarily.

He struggled to get up and regain his composure. Meanwhile, I could hear Austin screaming at the officer to get off me. The officer moved quickly, and suddenly, he and Austin were a tangle of limbs. When Officer Sanchez stood, he cuffed Austin. I had no idea what happened. I slowly got to my feet.

The officer turned to me. "Both of you will now be

going to the station," he said.

"Why?" I said before I could stop myself.

"Miss, you have to prove your identity," he said sternly.

"What did he do?" I nodded at Austin.

"Your friend attempted to interfere with police business." The officer sounded irritated. I could tell he was done answering my questions.

"Do we ride with you?" I asked.

Officer Sanchez nodded and led the way while everyone stood around looking shocked. Emily started to say something. I glared at her, and her mouth slammed shut.

Officer Sanchez loaded us into his car. It was my first time in a police car, and we both sat in the back seat. Austin still wore handcuffs, which was totally ridiculous.

"My dad is gonna kill me." My whisper sounded self-pitying.

"Will he come get me out?" Austin had a grin on his face.

"Why can't your mom?"

Austin laughed. "I'm gonna be here a while if we wait for my mom to bail me out."

* * *

"I tried calling you repeatedly." Regulus's voice was low and angry. "You could have called me."

Several feet separated us. I couldn't look into his eyes. "You sound like my dad."

"I thought something happened. I've been worried. And angry. I should have been there. Maybe you didn't want me to know what was happening." Now he seemed uncertain.

"I told you there was nothing you could do. We had it under control."

"So under control that you were in jail."

"I wasn't in jail. I was at the jail."

"And Austin?"

"Well..." I shuffled my feet. "He was in jail. But it was a misunderstanding."

I finally forced myself to look up and realized that Regulus wasn't even looking at me. He had pivoted toward the woods, away from me. His back was straight and his hands clenched into tight balls.

"Not again."

"What? Not again?" I asked.

"No missions, investigating, leaving my sight. You are no good to the IIA if you're dead."

"I can't believe you said that. Is this the real deal? You're looking out for the IIA?"

He turned toward me, came closer. "I can't stand it. This feeling I have makes me say the wrong things. Think the wrong things. I completely understand the need for the rules of interaction." He drew me into his arms and buried his face in my neck.

I breathed out in relief. I didn't want to fight. I always waited for the touching, the feeling I craved when I looked at him or talked to him.

"I do not know what to do with you," he murmured against my hair. "I don't know what to do with my feelings. So, I turn to what I know. I know how to be a team leader. And I fail in every other aspect."

"No. I know you were worried sick. Your instincts were correct. Bleeker is in Goliath."

"I suspected it." Regulus lifted his head to look at me. He kept his arms loosely around me. "He didn't hide very well."

"I know why he's there. There's a portal. I'm sure of it. I felt the draw of it. You didn't tell me there could be another one so close to us. I wasn't expecting that."

"It is surprising."

My dad's face appeared in the window, and he rapped on the glass from inside the house. Regulus dropped his hands.

"Five more minutes," Dad mouthed and held up his hand, fingers splayed. "Five."

"My dad isn't happy. He had to get Austin out." I waited for Regulus to ask me about that. When he didn't, I continued, "They said I was free to go, but Austin couldn't. His mom wouldn't answer the phone, so I called my dad."

Regulus appeared irritated. "This is probably his doing. He wanted to spend more time with you, so he landed you both in the jail." Then he laughed. "I know that's not true. I'm sorry that I said it."

"No, it's nobody's fault."

He again slid his arms around my waist. He bent to kiss me, but I angled my head slightly to one side, glancing to my left where the imposing figure of my dad stood, pulling back the curtain. Regulus stepped away, smiled, and waved at my dad.

"You can't go there again. It's too dangerous," he said. "Arizona and I can take care of Dr. Bleeker now."

"You're crazy if you think I'd let you go without me."

"You're crazy if you think I'd let you go." Regulus crossed his arms across his chest. He smiled.

"We'll see." I leaned forward to whisper in case my dad could hear me inside the house. "I don't think you can stop me."

The sound of a car coming up the drive interrupted Regulus's next retort. A shiny, candy-apple red Camry stopped in front of the house.

I jumped off the porch and ran over to the driver's window while squealing, "You are freaking kidding me! When did this happen?" I grabbed the car door to open it.

Em slung one foot out of the car and leaned out. "Hello there. How do I look? It's my color, right?" She flung her hair back and beamed.

"When?" I asked.

"My dad decided that it was time for me to have my own car since I got stuck with you and Austin last night." She couldn't stop smiling.

"You could have taken Austin's Jeep," I said.

"Are you kidding? I can't drive a stick. Besides, my parents said it was an early graduation present."

"Why do you get presents for graduating?" Regulus drew closer and inspected the inside of her new car.

Em and I stared at him. I turned to look at Em, hoping she'd say something that didn't sound entitled or spoiled. "Well?" I asked. "I'm not the one getting presents."

She squirmed in the seat, and I leaned down to sniff the new car smell. I couldn't help but inhale deeper and smile innocently at her.

"Um, I've worked hard in school, and this is a celebration kind of thing." Em's cheeks turned a flattering shade of pink. "Didn't you celebrate finishing high school?" she asked Regulus.

He gave her a blank face. "No," he said simply without elaborating. He never wanted to answer questions from Austin or Emily. He barely answered my questions. I had the distinct feeling that he was breaking every rule he'd been taught by disclosing anything about his life. His world.

"Then you can share my celebration," she said with that cheerful, I-don't-know-what-else-to-say-here look in my direction. She rose to exit the car and I backed up.

At that moment, the snarl of a motorcycle traveling up my gravel driveway interrupted the conversation.

I cocked an eyebrow. "Arizona, I assume."

"He was supposed to wait until I called him. I wanted to talk to you first." Regulus frowned and went to meet Arizona as the bike turned the last corner of the drive and came into view.

Arizona stopped the motorcycle and rested one foot on the ground before parking it and hopping off. Then he removed the helmet, shook his blond hair free from his face, and glanced at us with a lopsided grin.

"Looks like I didn't interrupt anything." Arizona smiled even broader. "Emily, Emily. I never guessed you might be here."

It was like he had built-in radar.

"And I never guessed you'd be here," Em replied.

"We're both lucky then, aren't we?" Arizona sauntered to the car and circled it. "Very nice, Em. Where shall we go first?" he asked, clearly including only Em.

I looked at Regulus and grinned, then turned to Em. "Yeah, where are you taking Arizona?"

"You guys want to go for a ride or not? My parents said I have to be back in a couple of hours." Em's voice shook with excitement. A pink glow emanated from her that I knew only I could see.

"I'm grounded," I said with regret. My dad stood in the window watching us. Even from a distance, I could see his arms were folded. I hadn't been grounded for years. The last time I'd been grounded, Pete and I had fought over who had to wash dishes after a dinner meal. We'd scuffled in the kitchen with Pete holding me in a headlock and giving me a bloody nose. We had both been punished.

"I have things to do." Regulus sighed and looked back at the window. He again waved at my dad. My dad waved back. Regulus left, his motorbike emitting what seemed like a frustrated roar.

"It looks like it will be the two of you," I said.

"Oh, that's OK. We can do it some other time," Em said. She looked at me and not Arizona.

"I'd love to go, Emily. Unless you're scared of being alone with me." Arizona was already sidling toward her car's passenger door. "We can go to that overlook on the mountain. You know...the secluded one." He winked at me.

"I c-can't—" Em stuttered.

"He's kidding. You guys could go get ice cream or something," I said helpfully. "The Dairy Barn has great strawberry sundaes."

"That sounds absolutely delicious," Arizona said in what I considered his sexy voice.

He was making Em nervous, and I wanted to throttle him. "Maybe you two should ask Tiny to go."

Arizona had met Tiny on a couple of occasions. I had no doubt that he didn't care for Tiny...or his easy relationship with Em.

"I'll behave," he said in a defeated voice.

"We'd better go before Mr. Taylor comes outside." Em waved at Dad, still in the window. He returned the wave but didn't budge from his post.

"'Bye, you guys. Sorry I'm missing out," I said.

"Me too. Me too," Arizona said with a note of sarcasm as he quickly got into Em's car.

I watched them leave without really wondering what they would talk about or do together. My main concern was where Regulus had gone and what he was doing.

Chapter Twelve

Grounded

I wanted to be trusted more than anything else in the world. Any day of the week, I could look my dad in the eye with no guilt. No regret. Today would be different. The grounding had been bearable for the first part of the week. School during the day and catching up on homework at night gave me the activity I needed to forget about missing Regulus. Dad let me keep the cell phone under the condition that I wasn't allowed to call or text anyone but him...and he planned to check my log.

On Wednesday, I stared out the window in Senior English mistaking another dark-headed guy for Regulus. Of course, it wasn't him and couldn't be him. The closed campus at Whispering Woods High mandated that all visitors register with the office personnel and have permission to be on campus. Regulus would never come to campus.

I bent my head again and tried to concentrate on my journal entries. Everything that popped into my head to write revolved around Regulus. I wrote something down and promptly began erasing. Write, erase, write, erase. My paper was worn and tired of my indecision and inability to focus.

Finally, Em offered to call Regulus and relay a note. My sour mood must have been more than she could stand. I scribbled a note to Regulus and handed it to her at the end of the day while we stood beside our lockers. Several students loitered in the hallway, talking in a bevy of blue boisterous voices.

I leaned in to whisper to Em. "Tell him that it has to be after ten. Not any sooner. And tell him that I'll put my lamp in the window. Like Paul Revere." I handed her the note. "No, wait. Not like Paul Revere. There's no way he'll know what that means." I was nervous at the thought of sneaking out or in. It was cold outside. I told myself several times that it made more sense for Regulus to come in. We'd freeze to death standing around in the windy night.

"I've got it. Quit worrying. How's he getting to your window?"

"Ladder," I said. "I'm leaving it on the ground on my side of the house. It's all in the note you're supposed to read to him. OK?"

"I can give him the info. You make sure you don't get caught. Winter formal is next weekend," Em said.

"Don't worry. I've got this planned out like a military invasion." My nervous laugh bubbled up, threatening to escape.

"I've got your back. You be ready, General Taylor."

"Thanks, Em. I know I can always count on you.

You're the best."

"I know." She smiled and turned. Glancing back at me one last time, she said, "But you'll owe me for this one."

"You got it."

I exhaled and reached for my books.

* * *

Dad kissed my forehead in the same way he had every night of my life for as long as I can remember. He patted my head and said, "Sleep tight. Don't let the bedbugs bite."

I watched him leave my room. Though I'd wanted him to hurry and go to bed, I said, "Dad?"

He came back, leaned down, and straightened the covers coming untucked at the bottom. He smiled tiredly. "What, Mia?"

"Are you lonely? I mean..." I stopped because I couldn't think of a way to finish. Heat crept up my neck and flooded my cheeks. "I want you to be happy."

"I'm happy, Mia. I don't know why you would even ask." He sat on the edge of the blanket that he'd tidied. Patting the top of my foot, he added, "I know you're feeling down about being grounded. I can't let you run wild—"

"I know that. This isn't about me."

"What is this about, then?"

"You never date. You go to work and then you're here."

"I have friends I work with. I'm not seventeen. They don't come to the house."

"Oh." I traced the pattern on my comforter. "Are you saying you've dated and I didn't know?"

"I wouldn't say dated." He tilted his head back. "I've gone out to dinner with a few women. I meet people who work on a project with me. Nothing serious. Nothing I should have told you about."

"Good."

"Good that there's been no one serious, or good that I've been on a date?"

"I don't want to think about you being lonely. I have friends, but I never see yours."

"Hmm," he said, nodding. "Sometimes, Mia, adults don't need the same things."

"Don't treat me like I'm a kid. I'm seriously worried about you. I want you to have someone in your life besides me."

"Seriously, there's been no one I've been that interested in since your mother left."

"She ruined you. Right?" I attempted to keep my tone even. I didn't want him to deny it automatically.

"Ruined... Do you want to talk about your mother?"

"Not particularly."

"You never ask about her. Don't you want to know why she left?"

"No."

"I think you need to know."

Silence. He was better at waiting out a topic in a conversation. I hated the silences more than the talking.

"Tell me then. It won't change what I think about

her. But you can tell me if it makes you feel better."
I pulled the blanket up to my chin.

"Your mom loved you and Pete very much."

My mouth dropped open. "Oh, please. Don't start with that." I moaned. "Actions speak louder than words."

"Mia—"

"Tell me why she left. Please. The truth. I'm a big girl. Was it an affair?"

"She told me that she was unhappy. That she needed to find her way." He stopped. After several moments, he began again. "She said that she couldn't take you and Pete from me. That she loved you both, but this life wasn't enough."

"She could have sacrificed and stayed. Plenty of people do that. She was selfish and didn't deserve you." I had chewed on my thumbnail until it was sore and throbbing. I forced my hand away from my mouth and took his hand in mine.

"No. She didn't need to stay. It would have made us all miserable. I watched her change after you were born. Every day, she was a little more on edge. Restless. I thought it was the post-partum blues. Maybe it was. In any case, I couldn't convince her to stay. After she'd been gone a year, I got served the divorce papers. I knew before then that she wasn't coming back."

"Good riddance."

"No, Mia. She'll always be your mother. You can't hate her. She couldn't live this life, but that isn't a reason to hate her. Nancy was isolated in the woods. She didn't have friends or family besides us. I met her when she was here taking soil samples for a research project she was working on. She hadn't planned to stay."

"I'll never understand how you can defend her. Why you don't hate her? It doesn't make sense."

"I might have hated her when she left, but I've gotten past that. There's a thin line between love and hate. It's easy to cross that line. Love is a much better side to be on." He leaned forward and pushed hair out of my eyes. "I'll always love my little girl no matter what she does."

I fought back the lump in my throat and the prickly feeling in my eyes. "I love you too, Dad." My voice came out in a croaky whisper.

I rolled over, and he walked out the door, quietly shutting it behind him.

* * *

At the gentle tap at the window, Biscuit growled, instantly alert. Grabbing the bag of dog cookies from my nightstand, I waved one at him, getting his full attention. "Shh. Biscuit, here."

Regulus had completed the window repair from the earlier break-in. A slim gap at the bottom showed it wasn't fully closed, allowing him to pry up the window. He slid the glass open in one easy motion.

"Hello," he murmured. Balancing on the ladder with acrobatic ease, he reached across the windowsill. "Did you find it necessary to risk my life by summoning me here to your bedroom?"

"I don't know what you're talking about," I

whispered. A thrill of excitement buoyed me. This would be the first time I had snuck someone into my room. I mentally argued that it was necessary. Desperate circumstances call for desperate measures, and I was desperate to see him.

Regulus climbed through the open window. "Your father," he said. "He's here."

I nodded. "He sleeps through everything. He won't wake up."

My room had chilled considerably in the few moments before he shut the window softly. I closed the distance between us and wrapped my arms around his waist. His clothing was cold from the temperature outside, but I pressed my head to his chest, nevertheless seeking warmth.

He relaxed and kissed the top of my ear. "You feel that you are safe because your father is downstairs, yet you tempt me beyond reason. You think—"

"I missed this," I said as I lifted my head to look into his dark blue eyes, the color of the deepest part of the ocean.

He smiled his rare, crooked smile and kissed the tip of my nose. Between each breath he took, he dotted kisses on another part of my face—my eyelids, my forehead, my lips. He lightly touched his lips to mine and then we were kissing. The familiar taste of his mouth, my heart beating in my ears, the solid feel of his body—all these things had become so important to me. I would never get tired of the bliss that surrounded my brain and made me forget everything else in the world.

When he stopped kissing me, everything in me wanted to protest. Before him, I had no idea what the big deal was. No idea why girls my age talked endlessly about guys they wanted to date. And sometimes they talked about guys they wanted to marry.

Now I got it. I wanted a marathon of kissing and more. It was a sweetness that filled me from the inside, including my heart.

"I only came because I needed to talk with you." He inched back to the desk and sat on it, crossing his arms.

"What if I don't want to talk?" I teased. Then, I saw the nervousness shimmering from him. Regulus normally exuded a warm yellow glow, like the sun at the end of a fine day in June. Tonight I noticed the magenta tinge of color when he spoke.

"You have been asked to report to The Vault. To meet the Makers. To accept your chip implant." His guarded look exasperated me. "To vow your allegiance."

"I thought I had time to decide about that. The chip." My knees shook, and I forced myself to sit on the edge of the bed. "You know...it will make it hard to get through airport security. My grandma has a steel bolt in her ankle and she has to go through this hassle—"

"No detection in airports," he said. "It's not made of steel or metal."

"Oh." I looked around my room because I didn't want him to see the fear that rose in my throat and chest like the foam on the surface of a boiling pot.

"There is no reason to be frightened. Unless you are changing your mind about things."

"I'm not changing my mind about anything. I saw

what Dr. Bleeker did. I'm all for stopping murderers and..."

"And?"

"I want to help you and Arizona. I can do that without the chip." I knew he believed I was being stubborn. But the situation reminded me of getting my shots when I was a kid. I'd known I had to do it, but I'd built up this intense dread beforehand.

It would be over quickly. Regulus told me that it didn't hurt. I trusted him.

"It isn't a rule you can debate, Mia. The time has come, and we will plan it for the next week your father is away. The implant of the chip is for our safety...for your safety. With it, I'll always know where you are and vice versa."

"And the IIA," I said.

He stared at me. "Yes. The IIA as well."

"Even my dad doesn't know where I am every minute. Why should the IIA?"

He groaned. "You ask why and I tell you. I give you all the answers I have and you keep asking for more." He paused. "Do you know what I think?"

I shook my head, afraid of what he might say.

"That you ask because you are doubting me."

"No. You know that's not true. I do trust you."

"Trust means you do something when you don't have all the answers."

"OK then. I'll do it. My dad leaves for Chicago the week after the winter dance. I can do it then. I'll miss a day of school."

I watched the relief spread over his face like the sun rising. It washed him in brilliant color, and his happiness was almost tangible, as though I could have touched it.

"You will be one of us then. Officially."

I grinned and threw my arm around his neck. I tiptoed and pulled his head down to meet mine. "You're finally making an honest woman out of me. Is that what's making you so happy?"

He looked confused.

"I mean, you want me to be officially with you guys. Right?"

"I want to make sure that you are one of the IIA and never to be mistaken for the enemy. It's protection for you to be part of my team."

"And we can always find each other."

"Yes. We can always find each other."

The moments between talking and kissing were always a blur for me. Once we started kissing, I lost all track of time and place. His lips felt exactly right.

Then he drew back. "This is not a good idea." He glanced around my dim bedroom with half-lidded eyes. "The chip won't matter if your father kills me when he discovers that I am in your room."

"He won't." I groaned while trying to pull his warm body back to mine. "I promise."

Regulus smiled with a tinge of regret. "I always calculate the odds and the risk is high. There will be another time and place for us." He smoothed my hair back and cupped my face in his palms for one last kiss. "I will do anything to protect what I have with you. I..."

My heartbeat pounded in my ears. I exhaled. "What?"

"It's all different now." He leaned his forehead against mine. "There is no plan for this, and I am having a difficult time creating one that will work."

"Plan for us?"

"Yes," he whispered. "A plan for us to be together."

He withdrew from me and turned. Biscuit followed him to the window. I grabbed Biscuit's collar. Regulus climbed through the window and pulled it down as he left. His last, beautiful smile warmed me, and I tingled from head to toe. I lay back on my bed, and Biscuit jumped onto the pillows. He scratched around making a nest for himself on one side and settled to sleep. I stroked his head and closed my eyes, thinking of what would have happened if Regulus had stayed.

Chapter Thirteen

Winter Wonderland

"When it says 'no high slits,' what does that mean exactly? High as in you can see my undies or high as in above my knee?" Em waved the paper above her head as she entered the door of my bedroom. "No bare midriffs. No revealing bustlines. No exposed bra straps." She flung herself onto my bed. "No, no, no. Do you see one 'yes' on this paper? No. They want us to come in some kind of dress that doesn't exist. Maybe something my gramma would wear."

I nodded and lay down next to her on the bed, then leaned over to grab a package of chocolate cookies. I set the bag between our bodies. We stared at the ceiling while devouring them.

"My mother bought my dress months ago. Before I even had a date. I didn't even say I was going, but she bought me a dress." Em munched her cookie for a moment before she added, "She bought more than one dress."

"Wow." I looked at her sideways. "Do you like them?"

"I don't know. They're her style. I'd say this paper could have pictures of my dress to illustrate what not to wear. I'll be lucky if they let me in the door after the chaperones take one look at me."

"Hmm," I said. "I'm sure it'll be fine." I could tell she was anxious.

"You don't have a dress yet, do you?" she asked.

"No." My answer came out unconcerned, but I had started to worry about it. I looked at some websites earlier in the day wondering if it was possible to order dresses like that with rush delivery. Answer? Yes. Had I done it? No.

"You have to wear one of mine then." She seemed happier, with a warm pink glow that suffused her cheeks and aura.

"Gee, thanks. Want me to get kicked out too?" I laughed.

"Sure. What are friends for if not a little mutual banning from the winter formal?" Em's voice was very serious. "I'll pick everybody up. We'll go in together. The four of us."

"You're not worried about going with Arizona, are you?"

"No." She drew the word out a little too long. "Of course not. I mean, what's there to be nervous about?"

"I wasn't sure you'd say yes when he asked you."

"Are you kidding? He's gorgeous. And he's funny.

How could I say no?"

"Em...if something about him bothered you, you'd tell me, right? I'm your best friend. I know when you're acting funny."

"It's all good. OK?" she said, brushing my question aside. "I've solved your dress problem. I'm better than the dang fairy godmother in Cinderella."

"If one fits."

"Fuchsia, aqua, red, or black? What do you think?"

"You have four freaking dresses? Your mother is out of..." I stopped myself from saying more.

At least her mother was around to buy dresses.

"Yeah. She is." Em grinned and shoved another cookie in her mouth.

"Your mom won't care if I wear one?"

"If she knew you didn't have one, we'd be shopping right now for yours. She lives for this."

"It's a good thing." I crossed my arms behind my head. "I'll still need shoes." I looked at my feet and stuck one bare foot beside Em's. I wiggled my naked, beat-up toes beside her pedicured ones. "Hmm."

She nodded.

"Your feet are tiny. How do you walk on those things? It's a shame you didn't ever get grown person feet," I teased.

"My mother is a Bigfoot like you. We'll raid her closet."

"If it weren't for you and your Bigfoot mother, I'd be nude at the dance."

Em held up the paper. "Against the rules. No nude attendees." She giggled. Sitting up, she grabbed my hand. "Come on. Let's go to my house and try some on."

She tugged but I didn't move.

"We're almost the same size. If the dresses fit you, they'll fit me."

I moaned. This was why I didn't have a dress yet. The thought of trying on and modeling possible choices rated right up there with cleaning my toilet or clipping Biscuit's toenails.

"You can't wait until Saturday night. Come. Now." She tugged harder and I relented.

* * *

Dad let me try on dresses at Em's house even though I was grounded. I'd mentioned the Whispering Woods Winter Extravaganza to him, but I'm sure that it hadn't crossed his mind that I'd need something special to wear. But he wasn't negligent. If I'd mentioned needing a new dress, he might have called my Aunt Candy or my grandmother for advice. He probably would have offered to take me to a mall. The fact that I could borrow a dress from Em seemed to be the answer to both our prayers.

Em's bedroom was white and pink with a wicker rocking chair in one corner, the same decor she'd had since she was four. I didn't know Em when she was four, of course. But she'd once told me that she loved her room. Em's mom had offered to change it, but Em said it was fine as it was. I figured she wanted to leave it alone purely because her mother wanted to update it.

While I waited for her to try on the dress she planned to wear, I clicked through songs on her iPod. Hooked up to Bose speakers, it sounded great, and I was amazed and a little jealous. She took all this for granted. I looked at the formal dresses hung in a display from the top of Em's closet door.

"My dad told me some stuff about my mom," I blurted and continued to scroll through her iPod.

"Your mom?" Em ran over with the dress gathered around her waist. One hand held the top of the pink dress in place while the other reached for the volume control on the speaker.

With the music all the way down, I answered in a small, self-conscious voice. "Yeah. You heard me right."

"Has she been in contact with your dad?"

"No," I said, surprised. "Why would you think that?"

"He never talks about her, does he?"

"No. But I brought it up."

"And?"

"He doesn't hate her like he should. He defended her when I said that." I motioned for Em to turn so I could zip her dress.

"Maybe he wanted out of their marriage too."

"No. I almost think he still loves her. I don't get it. If he knew that she's part of this thing I'm involved in, that she almost killed me—"

Em spun around. "Oh, Mia. You can't tell him."

"Of course I'm not gonna tell him. Do you think I'm nuts?"

She shrugged.

"I don't get what he saw in her. She's evil, and

she's working for Bleeker."

"Maybe something changed. Don't you find it strange that she's hooked up with Bleeker? How would she know him? Didn't she move a long time ago? The coincidence in all this is...too coincidental." Sometimes, Em's brilliance amazed me.

I sat dumbfounded. "She's a portal finder." I spat the words out.

Em jumped, then went to the full-length mirror in the opposite corner of her bedroom. "That makes sense. Didn't Regulus tell you that you and Pete both have the gift? You probably got it from your mom." She wasn't facing me, but she looked at me in the mirror. "What do you think?" She pointed at the dress.

I frowned. I didn't want to get anything from my mother. The thought made me squirm. Actually, I wanted to scream and throw things. "You're a sexy beast in it," I said, making a lame attempt to inject some enthusiasm into my voice.

She smiled. "Yeah. OK. Maybe they'll let me get by with it. I've got a lace thing I can wear over it until we get inside. Your turn." She motioned for me to try on a dress.

"Maybe she had something going on with Bleeker," I said. "A fling or something. Who knows?" I stood and pulled my T-shirt off over my head, then shimmied out of my jeans. I grabbed the dress closest to me—it happened to be the aqua one—and held it up, trying to figure out the best way to get into it.

"Over," she said, pointing at the dress. She grabbed the hem and lifted it, and I put my arms in the air so she could put it over my head.

"It doesn't matter why she is working for him. I really don't care," I said through the fabric of the dress as Em tugged it over my body. My head surfaced again and I let my arms down. I shooed her hands away and adjusted the thick bodice.

Em squealed. "Oh my gosh! You look like the little mermaid." She grinned.

Her annoying enthusiasm emerged in a glow of hot pink excitement. I had no idea what I looked like, but I definitely didn't want to look like a cartoon figure. I walked to the mirror. The person staring back was a stranger. A bona fide girl.

Em and I both stared in silence. Then my gaze met hers. She looked so happy it was ridiculous.

"Maybe I should just make the duct tape dress I saw online," I said awkwardly.

"You are wearing this dress if I have to make you keep it on until Saturday night." Em's words gushed out. "Seriously. If you want to try on the others you can, but—"

"No. I guess I can wear this." The words came out sounding a tad ungrateful even to me. I didn't mean it that way. I felt weird, and I couldn't sound like myself. I half expected my voice to trill in a musical little mermaid voice. I did sort of look magical.

"You could wear your hair up, but I like it down. Or we could roll it—"

"Don't get carried away, fairy godmother," I said. "I'm not doing anything crazy with my hair."

"OK, then down." Em leaned forward and arranged my hair over my shoulders. She met my eyes in the mirror. "Regulus isn't going to recognize you. You look so pretty."

I frowned.

"You know what I mean," she said.

"Yeah, I know what you mean." I smiled at her and gave her a hug. "Thanks, Em."

* * *

At 9:00 p.m. on Thursday night, rapping at the front door woke my dad from a snooze in his favorite recliner. At the sound, I flew down the stairs in a panic to beat him to the door without waking him. I was too late.

"You can't have company. You know you're grounded," he said crankily as he managed to get out of the chair and hobble over to block my view of the front door.

I could see Regulus through the oval window of the front door. I hopped from one foot to the other. "One second, Dad. One second. Something must be wrong because he knows I can't see him until Saturday night."

"Rules are rules. I've bent too many of them and you do whatever you want—"

"Daddy, please." I clasped my hands together. "Five more minutes. You can time it. You know him. He wouldn't come over if—"

Regulus again rapped on the door, staring through the glass at us.

"Five minutes, Mia. No more. I'm timing."

"Thanks!" I ran to fling the door open and step into

the porch.

"Mia," Regulus whispered. "I need to talk with you."

"What's up? I have exactly five minutes." I nodded my head toward my dad, whose silhouette could be clearly seen through the door glass.

Regulus hadn't shaved. His hair was also slightly wild like he'd been riding his motorcycle without a helmet. He still looked great, and my wandering thoughts made me smile.

"I've changed my mind about the chip. I've found another way. A better way for us."

"What are you talking about? Slow down." I led him to the porch swing and out of my father's line of sight.

"They were pressuring me to have your chip implanted. I thought it was the only way. But now I know of a man who can remove my chip. We can disappear. Together." He grabbed my hands in his and stared into my eyes. "We can be together."

"You're scaring me." I tried to stay calm. Regulus always appeared so steady and sure of himself. Tonight, his voice sounded uncertain. Worse, the usual warm glow of yellow that was part of being Regulus to me was more of a pink. Watermelon pink. "We're together now, aren't we? Besides, I told you I would get the chip. I trust you."

"I was wrong then. I was desperate."

"Why were you wrong? You said the chip would let us take care of each other. That we'd know each other's locations based on those signals. That's what it does, isn't it?"

"Part of it." His mouth formed a hard line. He

wasn't looking at me either.

My dad tapped on the window and pointed at his watch.

"I have to report to the Vault tomorrow. I wanted to see you and tell you that there is an alternative."

"Why do you have to go to the Vault?" I asked. "Is Arizona going too? You know the winter formal starts at seven. Em's going to drive and pick us all up." I felt like a heel for bringing it up. He obviously had bigger things to worry about than my high-school dance.

"They just ordered me to report, and I have no choice. I will be back in time. Don't worry."

I shrugged and smiled. "I wish I could go to the Vault with you."

The front door opened.

"I take you with me everywhere. In here." He placed his hand over his heart.

The statement took me off guard, and I gasped.

My dad stuck his head out the door. "Regulus," he said and gave a nod.

"Mr. Taylor," Regulus answered. "I apologize. It was important or I would have waited. I'm leaving town and didn't want Mia to worry about the dance. I'll be back."

"Oh," Dad said. "That's all right, but her time is up. She needs to come inside now." He then ducked back into the house.

"Are you sure everything is OK? I think you're worrying about this chip thing and that I'm not committed to you and the IIA, but—"

He placed his fingers on my lips. "I have been very confused. I haven't known what to do with these odd feelings. I think I know now." He smiled and leaned forward to quickly touch his lips to mine. "Did my heart love till now? Forswear it, sight! For I ne'er saw true beauty till this night."

"What?" I stared at the smile that had spread across his face. I stopped breathing. Never in my entire life had I been so happy.

"Brilliant man named Shakespeare. Romeo and Juliet. I read it this week in my lit class." He backed away from me and stumbled toward the porch steps.

I giggled.

He jumped off the porch, skipping the steps. "My heart loves now, Mia Carina Taylor. It is all very clear to me."

He stepped into the darkness. Moments later, I heard the motorcycle engine rev to life. He was gone.

* * *

I'd made a mistake. A terrible, horrible mistake.

I stood on a footstool trying for a better view in my dresser mirror. The dress was too tight, too shimmery, too aqua, too...not me.

"Mia, you all right in there?"

"Yeah, Dad. Fine. I'm fine," I muttered.

He knocked. "Can I come in?"

"No! I look like a..." I couldn't finish the sentence. I hopped off the stool and sat on my bed.

"I'm coming in."

I didn't turn around. Staring at the poster on my wall, I said, "I look ridiculous."

The door creaked as it opened. "Let me be the judge of that. Stand," he said. "Please."

The strapless dress fit snugly from bust to thigh, where it billowed into a mass of transparent layers of silk and taffeta, sweeping the floor.

"Dad, I can't go out in this. I don't know what I was thinking."

"Hmm," he said. "The truth." He motioned me to stand and spin around. He grinned. "Where's my little tomboy? You'll break a few hearts in that tonight."

"Daaaad." I groaned.

"Regulus is one lucky guy to have you as a date. He'd better not leave your side or someone will try to steal you away."

"Is it too tight? Do you think it's too—"

"It's perfect, Mia. Sweetheart, I don't know how Emily pulled this off, but the dress is made for you. I expect you to be lovelier only on your wedding day." His eyes twinkled.

The doorbell rang.

"It's Em. Are you sure I look OK?"

He nodded, eyes shiny. To my horror I thought he might cry.

"I gotta go, Dad."

"Be safe tonight, Mia."

"Thanks for forgetting about the grounding tonight."

"I love you, sweetheart."

"Love you too, Dad," I said as I teetered to the stairs in my high heels, grabbed the gown's hem, and managed to make it down.

* * *

The car was already warm from Em's drive over. Adjusting masses of taffeta, I settled into the passenger seat. "We're going to get the guys now?"

Em ignored me. "Listen, look in the back seat and you'll see a fur wrap. My mom said you have to wear it."

"Sure." I turned down the radio. "I tried to call Regulus today and he never answered. Have you talked to them?"

"Yeah, to Arizona," she said.

"Oh," I said, disappointed that Regulus hadn't called.

"They're going to meet us there."

"Why? Can't we swing by and get them?"

"Something about last-minute adjustments," she muttered. She turned up the radio. "You look great. My mom said she picked that dress out with you in mind."

"Whatever," I said, grinning. "I thought my dad was gonna cry before I left. He was so happy to see me in a dress."

"Aw," she said. "Your dad is the sweetest." She unwrapped a piece of gum while steering with her elbows. "Let's have fun tonight."

"I can't wait to see Regulus."

Chapter Fourteen

Reunion

A pastel explosion of color covered every inch of the Whispering Woods High gymnasium. At least a hundred pounds of glitter and billions of tiny white lights twinkled on artificial tree branches. I followed Em underneath the hulking arch that proclaimed Enchanted Forest.

"What happened to the steampunk theme I voted for?" I looked around. "It's like we fell into a bag of taffy."

"Pretty, isn't it?" She ignored my scowl.

"What's this supposed to be?"

"Fairy-tale night. Like Cinderella and Snow White."

"Hmm," I said, still not seeing what the decor had in common with children's stories of wicked stepmothers and evil witches.

"Come on. I think I see Arizona. I gave him the passes so they could get in."

I let her grab my hand and lead me through a crowd of dancers. Looking down at my dress, I held my breath. It was silly to be nervous about seeing Regulus. About him seeing me in the dress.

I took a deep breath and opened my lids slowly in anticipation.

"Hi, beautiful." Austin stood inches from me in a black suit. He smiled, and I smiled back. "You look incredible."

"Thanks," I said and noticed Arizona, already holding Em's hands, standing at Austin's right. Everything seemed to move in slow motion as I looked in confusion at Arizona, then Em, then Austin.

"Where's Regulus?" I said. I even turned to look behind me.

"Listen, Mia, he really wanted to be here, but..." Arizona twitched with nervousness. "He tried."

"He tried what? I don't get it. Where is he? And Austin, why are you here? Did you bring somebody from school?"

"I called Austin and told him to come along. Or you'd be alone," Arizona's tone was apologetic.

I didn't care. "You what? This isn't football, Arizona. You don't send a fresh player in."

Em put her hand on my arm.

I shrugged it off. "Did you know about this?" My voice rose, and people were starting to stare. I knew I was throwing a tantrum but couldn't stop myself. "You knew. You did," I said as I backed away. The betrayal made me feel like my heart was catching on fire.

"Mia, he couldn't make it back, and...we didn't want this night to be ruined." Arizona waved his hands, trying to calm me down, I guess.

"I would have been fine if he'd called to tell me this." I backed up two more steps. I could see the disappointment on Austin's face, and it made me angrier. How could Regulus send another guy in his place if he cared that much about me?

Austin caught me by the arm. "Mia, you're overreacting. I'll take you home if you want."

"Yeah, that's what I want. I'm sorry, Austin. Take me home, OK? I hate these things. It was a stupid idea for me to come anyway."

"Sure." Austin glanced over at Em. "You all right?"

"Yeah. Go ahead." She turned to me. "Mia, don't be mad. I didn't know until the last second. Promise."

"Thanks for the dress," I said stiffly. "I'll return it tomorrow."

Austin took my elbow and steered me toward the exit. Once outside, we went to the parking lot.

"I'm happy I came," he said.

When I didn't respond, he continued, "It's a good thing because I've never seen you in a dress like that before."

I looked at him, confused. I couldn't imagine why he was still being nice to me after I had practically thrown a screaming fit inside the building.

"I thought I liked being with you because you get me. And you're into the gaming. And you're real, you know." He paused. "I thought that was all it was.

That you're like a buddy. I was wrong."

I shook my head. "Huh?"

"I have news for you, Mia Taylor. You're not one of the guys." Austin dropped his hand from my elbow and walked in front of me. Then he turned to scrutinize me from head to toe. "I would never take you for granted, and I'd certainly never stand you up."

"Please take me home, Austin."

"Yeah, OK. But don't forget that I'm the one who really knows you and everything you want in life." He opened the door to the Jeep for me.

There was no way I could get up into the seat unless I planned to split the side of the dress. Austin obliged, grinning while lifting me into the passenger seat.

* * *

Still in the aqua dress, I flung myself down on my bed. I was in no mood to take time to undress. Throwing myself a pity party ranked high on my list of priorities at the moment. Dad seemed surprised when I got home so early, but he took one look at my face and didn't ask. I had never been as thankful.

Biscuit insisted on licking a path around my hairline and anywhere he could see skin. Eventually, he settled in beside me, and I turned my head to him.

"I was really bad," I said to him. He blinked and stuck out a pink tongue to lick my arm.

"I was so bad, Biscuit. My friends will never want

to do anything with me again." I sniffed and closed my eyes. Biscuit licked my cheek as a hot tear slid downward.

* * *

My cell phone vibrated. Biscuit gave a quick bark.

I peered in the dim light at the screen. It was Arizona.

"Hello."

"You OK?"

"Of course. Listen, I can't believe I acted like that. Like some spoiled brat. I'm sorry. I guess I was nervous to begin with since—"

"Mia."

"Yeah?"

"The portal has moved again. I need you to find it."

"Why didn't you say so?"

"It's bad timing. I should have gone with him, but he wouldn't let me. They said for him to come alone."

"I can find it," I said. I sat up and straightened the dress.

"Can we go now?"

"Sure. I'll change."

"No, I'm outside with Em. Let's go now." He sounded urgent.

I frowned. "In this dress? Is something wrong?"

"I can feel that Regulus is coming through."

I nodded in understanding even though he couldn't see me. The chip always made location of the team member possible. "Sure. I'll be right down."

I scooted off the bed and shoved my feet into my old Converse tennis shoes and grabbed the skirt of the dress so it wouldn't drag on the ground. At the last second, I snagged my jean jacket to put on. I looked at my ensemble of mermaid dress with tennis shoes topped by a clashing blue denim jacket and grimaced.

Tiptoeing down the stairs, I slipped past my dad in his recliner. His mouth hung open and a loud snore stopped me momentarily before I silently opened the front door.

Em and Austin weren't exactly at the door, but I could see a flashlight glowing halfway down the gravel drive. I ran to them, struggling to adjust my vision to the pitch-blackness of the night.

"Portal," Arizona demanded.

"Gimme a second. It's not like I flip a switch." I walked a couple of feet away from Em and closed my eyes to concentrate. There's nothing like having an audience when trying to block everything out. I listened to the sounds of the night and saw indigos and purples swirl past me in my mind's eye. I smelled the evergreen and wet leaves...

Sweetness filled me. Breathing in slow steady drafts of life force, I searched for the pull of the portal, allowing my feet to move of their own accord. "It's not far," I whispered. "It's actually closer and back near the waiting booth."

I opened my eyes and let myself be drawn like metal called by a magnet, hurrying through the dappled shadow and moonlight. The closer I came to the portal, the stronger the desire to meet it.

Arizona seized my arm, stopping me.

Regulus stood motionless in the clearing, silver light pouring down to illuminate his gleaming form.

I shook free. Grinning, I ran to him, no longer mad about his absence tonight or that Arizona had brought Austin in his place.

I came close enough to see his eyes glittering in the moonlight.

He cocked his head. "Halt."

Who was he talking to? I continued toward him, noting he had something in his hand. A shiny metal box, glittering in the moonlight.

"Mia!" Arizona shouted.

Pain shot through my head. My knees buckled. In a flash, I thought of the dirt that I'd get on Em's beautiful mermaid dress and of how the moonlight shafted down into the clearing like a spotlight.

I reached out to Regulus. Time stopped for one long second as I looked into his dark eyes.

Then, I thought no more.

* * *

Em was hovering over me with tears in her eyes. Her hands shook as she pushed hair off my forehead. Arizona's voice whispered somewhere in the background.

"It's all going to be OK. Don't worry," she said over and over.

My tongue was dry and sticky in a mouth that didn't cooperate when I opened it to speak. Em's usual pink glow was a fiery red haze that emanated from every pore. I stared at her.

I tried again.

"He zapped me." I giggled and said, "I must look crazy in this dress."

The corner of Em's mouth lifted slightly. She shook her head. "You look awesome in this dress." She looked behind her. "I'm sorry, Mia. I'm so sorry."

I raised my eyebrows, confused. What did she have to be sorry about? She wasn't the one who'd accidentally zapped me. Trying to sit up, I slapped her fussing hands away. "Geez, Em. Let me up."

She helped me stand. My head was spinning a little, so I kept a hand on her arm. A cloud drifted across the moon, and darkness smothered me like a heavy quilt. I noticed the silence, the pull of the portal, and the lack of the breeze I'd felt earlier.

"Regulus." I squinted at him.

He didn't answer.

"Regulus?" My voice came out in a wobbly whisper.

Then I saw him walking off, leaving the clearing without us. Leaving without checking to see if I was OK after he'd lit up my brain like a pinball machine.

"What's going on?" I tried hard to still the quiver in my voice.

Arizona looked from Em to me. He put his arms around me in a hug.

I pushed him away. "Tell me now."

"He's had a cleansing, Mia."

I shook my head. "I don't know what that means."

"The IIA cleansed him of certain memories." Arizona waited a moment. Lifting my chin, he looked into my eyes. "It's not you. They did something to him. I've heard about the procedure, but I've never known someone who—"

"What did they do to him?" I screamed.

"They took away certain memories. When he came through, he didn't recognize you."

"Me?" I couldn't breathe. My throat constricted into a tight vice, and the hammering of blood in my ears competed with Arizona's voice.

"Regulus stopped you because...he doesn't know who you are." Arizona looked over the top of my head. "I've told him that you're one of us, our portal finder... He remembers me and even remembers Em. They were very selective in what they took."

"Get out of my way. I'm more than your portal finder." I shoved Arizona aside, grabbed the skirt of my dress, hiked it high and started running. Cold air whooshed around my bare legs.

The fine material of my dress caught on brush that seemed to reach and snag me at every turn. Ripping sounds told me that I had totally ruined the dress. The thought made me laugh a little hysterically.

I rounded a corner and ran into Regulus.

Surprised he'd been standing still as if waiting for me to find him, I didn't know what to say. His shadowed face told me nothing.

I touched his arm.

He stared at my hand.

I took it away.

"Regulus." I hoped all he needed was to hear my voice.

"Did you need something?"

"Need?" I asked. "Need? Look at me."

Without moving, he looked at my face and my hair

and my torn aqua dress.

"Look at me and tell me you don't remember." Desperation poured from my voice. I was trying hard not to cry. I searched him for the warmth I usually saw. All I could find was a dark golden brown of irritation and impatience.

He met my eyes for a second and looked away. "I know you are the portal finder."

"It's me, Mia." I knew it was stupid to say it. Sometimes you can't stop yourself. His words had forced a bitter lemon taste into the back of my mouth. My mind was whirling as I tried to find something important to jolt his memory. Instead, I found myself setting my hands on his shoulders and edging closer.

He looked shocked and promptly stepped back.

My hands fell away.

"There are things I must do tonight." He turned and left.

My mind boggled. "What do you have to do?" I ran to follow him. Leaves crunched. Arizona and Em walked behind us.

"Hey, where are you going?" Anger was now taking over. My hands and legs were shaking. A new surge of adrenaline flowed through my body. "Did they also program you to be a rude jerk?"

Regulus stopped and stiffened. He glanced back. "Are you sure she is part of us?" he asked Arizona.

"She is," Arizona said. "She's upset."

"I'm right here," I said, exasperated. "I'm feeling like I've lost my mind, but I still have my hearing."

Regulus turned to me. "I am aware that certain histories have been deleted for me. I am not 'programmed.' Selective history deletion was necessary. It's a cleansing. I also know that I am in charge and you are not. Arizona, detain her. I need to get supplies together."

He turned away and left. Arizona gently took my arm. I tried to shrug him off, but he was stronger. Regulus was disappearing into the darkness quickly; he'd begun to run.

"This cannot be real," I said through gritted teeth. "How can you let this happen?" I asked Arizona.

"It's already happened." His voice was low and soft. Em had a pitying look on her face that made me madder.

Angry tears filled my eyes. "Did you know they were going to do it? That they would make me and Regulus disappear, like we never happened?" I wanted to blame someone even though I knew that it wasn't Arizona's fault.

"You need to stop worrying about you. There's something more going on. The IIA is sending Regulus on a mission alone. They never do that. We need to figure out what they've ordered."

"Why would they do that? Send him alone?" A thought flickered on the edge of my consciousness and broke free. "They think we'll stop him or refuse to go along."

Arizona studied my face. "I agree with you."

"I guess I can save my heartache for tomorrow." I sniffed and took a deep breath, calming myself.

"Thatta girl." Arizona made a fist and hit me lightly on the shoulder.

Em put her arm around me, smiling gently. "We'll figure it out. He's still him and you're still you. There are some things that can't be erased."

Despite my newfound clarity, a fat tear slid down one cheek. I brushed it away with the back of my hand. "I knew there was a good reason for not getting that chip." I smiled. "The IIA doesn't control me. I'll do what it takes to find Bleeker, find my brother..." I trailed off. "Find a way to turn back what they've done to Regulus."

"There's no turning back, Mia. Moving forward is the only way to get somewhere." Arizona nodded his head toward the road, then took off in a slow jog. Em and I followed.

Chapter Fifteen

Hidden Mission

When I was five, I tagged along with my brother everywhere. If he went to Cub Scout meetings, I was there. If he played baseball, I was there. He wasn't always happy to have me around and, as older brothers tend to do, he ignored me when he was with friends. I didn't mind. I knew he was just pretending. He'd be there if I absolutely needed him.

One time, some kid at the ballpark purposely knocked my snow cone out of my hands to fall in an icy heap on the bleachers below. Before I could even cry, my brother ran over and tugged that kid's hat off his head. "Sorry," he said unconvincingly to the kid. "Go buy my sister another one or I'll knock more than your hat off." My brother had been watching from the dugout.

That's what I kept hoping for with Regulus. He had to be pretending not to know me. With the IIA watching, he had to convince them they'd been successful. Mia Taylor, gone from the memory of their agent...forever.

"What time is it again?" I asked Em. I wasn't wearing a watch, and her car's clock said 6:00 p.m., which was obviously wrong.

"Five minutes since the last time you asked. Geez. I know how parents feel now." She adjusted her strapless bra underneath the bodice of her formal she still wore. "You look wild. Like you could be a model for some crazy magazine ad. Or you might be a bag lady."

I flipped down the sun visor and looked at myself in the mirror. She was right about the wild part. My hair, which I usually dried without hair product or styling, had been windswept into a mass of curls around my head. Slightly crunchy, sticky curls. I had started out the night with it up and had painstakingly used the curling iron to help me form tiny pin curls from strands of hair around my face. I now looked like I'd stuck my finger in an electrical socket. My mascara had smeared into raccoon smudges around my eyes since I hadn't been able to stop myself from crying. Between my tangled poof of a hairdo and my jean jacket thrown over the now tattered aquamarine-colored dress, I was the definition of mess. I also had on the black Converse tennis shoes that I'd grabbed from my room. They actually looked kind of cute with the outfit.

Em leaned forward to open the glove compartment. "Here's some baby wipes I keep for spills. Do something to your face."

I took the package she offered and removed a wipe.

"You're always so prepared." I began cleaning my entire face with the wipe. The car heater was starting to make me feel like I was in a sauna. "Arizona has been in there long enough to find out what he's doing." I chewed on my thumbnail. I took off the denim jacket.

"It's been fifteen minutes, Mia. Come on. Calm yourself."

"I am calm." I threw away the wipe and began to fidget with the heater vents, pointing them all away from me.

She sighed and turned down the airflow. "What's your curfew tonight?"

"Curfew? I don't care what it is." I stared out the window, which was becoming covered in condensation.

"I care. You'll be grounded forever at this rate."

"I'll text Dad and tell him that I decided to go back to the dance. He was asleep when I left. He originally didn't give me a time. He thinks it's a double date, so he's not worried about it. I told him I might spend the night at your house."

"Great. I'm your cover."

"You? Peggy Sue and Pops waiting up?" I grinned. Em wouldn't have a curfew.

Em gave me a dirty look. "I actually told her that I might crash at your house when I take you home."

The door to the dormitory at Whispering Woods U opened, and Arizona appeared. He wore jeans and a black T-shirt topped by a leather jacket instead of the tux. He opened the back door and got in.

"You freakin' changed clothes in there. That's what took you so long," I said to him.

"I had to have some excuse to be in the room. Otherwise, it would look like I followed him." He grimaced. "Listen up. Something is happening tonight. Regulus doesn't shut me out. It's not his way. I don't know how to explain to you how weird this is."

"Oh, I pretty much think that it's all weird, all the time," I said it in my best commercial voice. "It's a new motto for us."

"I'm glad you're OK." Arizona looked at me and set his chin on the back of my seat.

"OK is relative," I said without looking at him or Em. "I'll make it. At this moment, I'm just so pissed." My voice began to rise. "They had no right."

"It's the rules, Mia. We told you this." Arizona's voice was gentle. "I didn't think that they would find out." He stroked my hair like I was a little kid. The car was silent except for the hum of the engine and the heater. "He cared for you. He did. They might have ignored it if not for that."

"Thanks for nothing." I attempted a smile. My mouth rose at the corners, but the rest of my face refused to follow. "What do we do now?"

"I need all the reinforcements I can get. You two are in?"

"Duh," Em said.

"Yeah, duh." I managed a tiny smile.

"Will Austin talk to you again after tonight?" Arizona asked me.

"Yeah. I think so. Friends through thick and thin, you know." I didn't sound as sure as I wanted.

"Call him. I saw a map of Goliath on Regulus's printer. You're taking a road trip." Arizona smiled.

"You have any food in here, Emily?"

"Really?" Em said. "You have to eat...now?"

"My level of charm and intellect requires a constant source of calories."

"We can't go get food now. We'll lose him," Em said.

"He was getting in the shower a minute ago. It's his routine before he goes to bed. He's trying to throw me off."

Em shifted quickly into drive and sped out of the parking lot. "Drive-through," she mumbled. "Only with you would we interrupt this rescue mission for a fast-food emergency."

"Wait. You said, you're taking a road trip. As in us, not you. What about you? Aren't you going?" I said.

"I can't go, Mia. I want to more than anything, but he'll know I'm there. The IIA will know." Arizona held up his wrist with the chip implant. "I need to borrow Em's car. I have a plan."

I was finding my way out of the numbness. Picking up my cell, I hit speed dial for contact one. "Austin?"

"Yeah, babe." He sounded tired.

I let the "babe" part slide. "I need your help." I took a deep breath. "I really need it or I wouldn't ask."

"I know. When and where?"

"Now. We're sitting outside Regulus's dorm. When he leaves, we're going to follow him. We think he's heading to Goliath."

"You spying on the boyfriend?" I knew Austin was teasing since he didn't know about the cleansing. It still hurt.

"The IIA did something to him. Austin..." I said.

"Yeah?"

"He doesn't remember that he's my boyfriend. He doesn't remember me at all."

The silence on the phone seemed to stretch endlessly before Austin finally spoke. "I'm sorry, Mia."

"Sure," I said. "Right now, we think he's doing something he's been ordered to do alone. Arizona has a bad feeling about it. We're not letting him go alone."

"I'm coming." No hesitation or doubt.

I sighed. Austin was that friend you could call in the middle of the night. I was sorry that I'd never be more than that to him. He clicked off, and I put down the phone.

We drove into the drive-through lane of the local fast-food restaurant and ordered several burgers, fries, and shakes. My stomach had been a knot of emotion and stress, but I was suddenly famished. Arizona ate his order and asked to finish the remainder of mine. Em nibbled on her fries while driving and maneuvered into a dark corner of the dormitory lot with her lights off.

"This chip business. Does he know you're this close?" I asked.

"Yes." Arizona squinted to see someone walking across the north end of the lot. "I told him that we took you home and Em was waiting in the car for me."

"What does he think she's waiting for?" I asked, confused.

"What do you think we might do in a dark parking lot?" he asked, grinning widely.

Em threw a fry at him. "Um...you wish." She wasn't angry though. I could tell she thought it was funny.

My cell rang.

"I'm here. I didn't pull up. Where are you?" he said.

"Far end of the lot by the line of poplar trees," I said.

"South end of lot twelve," Arizona said simultaneously.

"You're on speaker phone now," I said as I held out the phone where Em and Arizona could hear.

"Do you want me to pull up there or what?" Austin said.

"No, they'll come to you. I'm keeping Emily's car. Where are you?" Arizona looked around.

"Admin building by the Dumpster," Austin said. "Tiny's with me."

"Keep your phone charged and on. Both of you. I can tell you if he's moving and the distance and direction. I can give you coordinates for him."

"Holy crap." I couldn't breathe. "Are you saying the chip has global positioning?"

"That's exactly what I'm saying. Bet you wish your portal finding was that exact," Arizona said, as if I should be jealous.

"No. I don't." Now I understood why the IIA wanted me to have it done. They'd know exactly where I was all the time. I had pictured it all differently. I sort of thought it worked like my portal sensing—an inexact science and more of a feeling than a geographical map.

"Why did you need my help in the woods?" I asked.

"The portal invalidates the signal. I would be able to locate him after he was already through but not before," Arizona said.

"Are you guys coming?" Austin cut in on us.

"Yes," I said. "We're on our way."

"Mia, take this." Arizona gave me a stunner.

"I haven't practiced enough," I said while trying to hand it back. "What if I accidentally kill someone?"

"Then you'll have to make sure you do it right." He pushed it back toward me and smiled. "I have faith in you."

Em and I opened our car doors as softly as possible. While trying to steal across the parking lot, I muttered an oath to never ever wear a dress again as long as I lived. Em had no trouble running in her winter formal ensemble. She even looked graceful.

I was winded when we reached the Jeep.

"Hola, ladies." Austin jumped out of the driver's side and stared at me, gaze traveling from my messy hair to the torn dress and tennis shoes. "What the hell happened to you?"

"Rough night," I answered, not wanting to explain all that had happened. "Could you save the gawking for some other time when I can deal with it?"

"We have to hurry," Em said. "I've got to download an app on my phone for GPS."

"Got it," Tiny said in his low gravelly voice while holding up his phone. "Trade phones with me, and I'll get your download started."

"Thanks, Tiny," Em said. "You're the man."

"Uh-huh." Tiny smiled.

I was amazed. I'd never seen him smile. "Let's get on the road," I said. "Arizona texted me. Regulus is moving."

Austin waited for us to hop in the back seat and buckle up. The heater air in the Jeep didn't reach the back seat, and I began to shiver.

Tiny shoved a jacket in my direction. "Take this. I can hear your teeth chattering from here, I stay hot anyway."

I gratefully took the jacket and spread it over Em's and my legs like a blanket. Watching my phone for texts, I read off coordinates. Tiny programmed in destinations while Austin made sure that we stayed in range but out of sight.

I felt my eyelids getting heavier by the minute and yawned as I laid my head back. The Jeep seat vibrated with movement, and I struggled to keep my eyes open.

"I've got it, Mia."

I heard the words and felt the phone being taken from my grip. I thought I'd rest my eyes for one minute. No more.

* * *

The brush of a hand on mine woke me. "We're here," Em said.

I looked through slitted eyelids to see that we were in total darkness and still in the Jeep. I must have fallen asleep. I immediately went into panic mode. Had I missed something important?

"Regulus went inside this building," Austin whispered as he pointed across the street at a brick building in the middle of what looked like an industrial area.

"This is Goliath?" I asked.

Tiny nodded while looking at his phone.

"We're not near the railroad tracks, are we?" I wanted to know.

"No. Why?" Austin said.

"I don't feel the portal here," I answered.

"Why do you think Regulus broke into this building?" Em said.

"Million dollar question," Austin said. "Man, I sure don't want to run into Officer Sanchez again."

"Oh." Em and I groaned in unison.

I leaned forward to talk to Austin. "You have to stay out of trouble. I don't know if my dad will come and bail you out a second time."

He shrugged. "Life is short and simple. I do what I have to do and worry about the consequences later."

"It's not simple," I said, an ache deep in my chest. "It's—"

"Shh," Tiny said and signaled at a large silver Hummer driving into the parking lot of the building. It parked at the corner of the building lit by a streetlamp.

"He's still in there," I said while panic threatened my ability to speak.

A man exited the driver's side, while behind him, a woman got out of the backseat.

Nancy Taylor.

When I finally tore away my mesmerized glance to look at the man, I recognized Dr. Eli Bleeker. A man almost as large as Tiny, he held something— probably a key card—and went to the building's front door.

Em laid her hand on my arm. "He'll hear them coming."

"He must have set off an alarm when he went in. Why else would they be here at this time of night?" Austin said. "Maybe we should call Officer Sanchez for backup."

"You've got to be kidding," I said.

"They're turning more lights on. I think they're searching the place," Austin said.

"How can you tell?" Em said doubtfully.

"I need to get out. I can't see what's going on." I grabbed the door handle.

"No, Mia, stop—" Austin's voice was urgent.

My shoes made no sound as I tiptoed to the front side of the Jeep and then sprinted to the building. I made it to the far corner away from the streetlamp when I noticed Em, Austin, and Tiny all following me.

"I didn't say to follow me," I whispered in a strained voice.

"Yeah? Well, we didn't tell you to run for the building like an idiot." Tiny was out of breath and looked like he wanted to strangle me. He was wearing only a faded concert T-shirt and jeans.

I edged to the shadowed side of the building. "Where's your jacket? It's thirty degrees out here."

"Somewhere in the back seat," Tiny hissed.

"Oh, and I'm the idiot," I said. I peered around the corner.

The parking lot was dead silent and still. Then I noticed something silver lying on the asphalt about twenty yards away.

Em mumbled something that I couldn't quite hear. "What?"

"It's my shoe. I dropped my shoe."

Looking down at her bare feet, I gasped. "For

crying out loud. What is your shoe doing out there?"

"I carried them so I wouldn't make noise." She shifted uncomfortably. She still clutched the other shoe.

"Everyone should stay very still." The voice boomed out of nowhere. I'd know the voice anywhere. It belonged to my former science project mentor, a man I'd trusted at one time. The man who had talked me into letting him go before I knew he was a murderer. Eli Bleeker.

Bleeker came toward us, handgun pointed. "My lovely Mia Taylor. I've been looking forward to seeing you again." He grabbed Em's arm. She whimpered a little, and I thought Tiny was about to come unglued. I shook my head at him.

Bleeker shoved the gun into Em's back. She gave us a reassuring smile. Just like Em to try and make us feel better.

"Let's all walk inside, kiddos. It's so cold out here." He shivered theatrically. "Walk to the entrance, and Miss Prom Queen and I will follow behind."

"Sure," I said. We obediently walked to the door. "We go in?"

"Yes, dear. Make yourself at home."

We entered single file. The bright lights were blinding, and I wanted to shade my eyes.

I tried to stay calm. I needed a plan, but I didn't know if they already had Regulus or not.

Bleeker kept Em in front of him, his human shield. He looked from Tiny to Em to me and then Austin.

"No shoes, no coat, no service..." he said with a serious face, and then started chuckling.

"I think that's no shirt." I stared at him.

He raised an eyebrow. "Maybe that should be no brain, no service. Did you really think you wouldn't get caught breaking and entering? You set off our security alarms. You're not very good at this."

I forced myself not to look at anyone. If Bleeker thought we'd tried to break in, then he must not know Regulus was inside. Now that my eyes had adjusted to the bright lighting, I could see that we stood in an antiseptic, bare lobby. An intercom on the wall next to a door, presumably leading inside to the guts of the facility, told me that security was paramount. A glass window beside the door allowed someone from the interior to see who stood in the waiting area.

"Is this where we ask to see the wizard?" I smirked. "To get a brain and all?" I was nervous that he still hadn't let go of Em.

"Mia, you're actually funny," Bleeker said. He wasn't smiling or laughing. "Do you want to fix this situation? You can, you know. You are actually the one who can make all this go away."

"Come again?" I asked.

"You could be very useful to me. Especially since Nancy is not very helpful to me these days. It's a hit-or-miss situation with her talent. On the other hand, you've made a huge mess by bringing your friends here." He tapped his forehead like he was thinking.

He suddenly jumped. Em squealed and the rest of us gasped.

Bleeker's excited face glowed. "Wait. I have a terrific idea."

We waited in silence. I could hear movement somewhere else in the building. Had Nancy Taylor found Regulus yet?

"Here's the new plan," Bleeker said. "I won't kill your friends in exchange for your services."

"What do I need to do?" I asked.

"You will lead me to the portal. Of course, your friends will have to go through."

"I don't understand. Why do they have to go into a portal?"

His mouth made a thin line. Em whimpered again, and I guessed he'd jabbed the barrel of the gun into her back.

"I am not stupid," he said, punctuating every word slowly. "They know too much and can't stay here. I would think living somewhere else is preferable to death."

"Oh, sure," I said, nodding. "That makes sense." I wanted him to calm down. The mossy green haze of colors emanating from his body told me that he was getting pissed and crazy.

"In here. I have them in the lobby," Bleeker yelled.

More noises sounded down the hallway. The interior door swung open. Nancy Taylor stood framed in the doorway wearing a black fitted turtleneck and black pants. She held a small gun and looked like she had walked out of one of my videogames. Two armed guard types were with her, but I only had eyes for her.

I couldn't stop myself glaring at her with hate pouring out of every cell in my body. When my gaze met hers, I could tell that the loathing was mutual.

She limped when she came toward us, and I smiled.

"Hello, Nancy," I said calmly. "How's the leg

treating you these days?" I pointedly studied the area where I'd stabbed her a couple of months ago with a letter opener.

Her expression told me she'd like to kill me right there. Her gun hand moved slightly, and her free hand tightened into a fist.

"Now, here, here. Let's play nice," Bleeker said to Nancy. Maybe he knew how close she was to blowing. I must have pushed the right buttons. I smiled wider.

Nancy took Em's arm and held the gun on her, freeing Bleeker. The two guards, also dressed in black turtlenecks like we were in a James Bond movie, flanked Tiny and Austin, presumably to escort them at gunpoint.

Bleeker came to my side and set a heavy hand in the small of my back. He smiled sweetly at me. Someone stupid might mistake us for great friends. "Come. I'm anxious to test your skills."

I nodded. Nervously glancing over my shoulder as we followed the others to the front door, I glimpsed movement on the other side of the glass window.

Regulus watched us from the shadows.

Chapter Sixteen

Pit Stop

The Hummer couldn't seat all of us, so Bleeker split us up, packing us into separate vehicles. I rode with Bleeker, who drove the Hummer. I sat shotgun; Tiny and the two guards were in the backseat. Although Tiny had failed to say even one word the entire time, his massive size must have pegged him as dangerous. And he had a murderous look on his face while he watched Em like a hawk.

I worried about Em and Austin with the crazy, gun-wielding woman in the Jeep following us.

"Mia. Where to?" Bleeker smiled pleasantly.

"Huh?"

"Portal. Concentrate." He adjusted the heat and turned around to address our passengers. "Everybody comfortable? Temp OK?"

Silence.

"Wonderful." Bleeker looked at me again. "What

can we do to help? Music? Or does it need to be quiet?"

"It doesn't work like that. I don't feel anything right now."

"And why is that? I'm very sure that you can locate it."

"It's like...I need to be closer. I can't hear my television at my house here either, you know." I waited for him to get it. "It's just too far for me to sense anything."

"Hmm. We'll drive around then until we are close enough."

"Wait," I said. I didn't think I could stand a road trip of the sights in Goliath. "I know it was near the railroad tracks at one point."

"Right, you found it during the weekend you were snooping around with the ghost hunters." He shifted into reverse. "Then off to the tracks we go."

He switched on the radio, and classical music wafted throughout the inside of the Hummer. I turned around to make sure the Jeep was following us. I couldn't see anyone inside, and I prayed that Austin and Em wouldn't do anything stupid. My mind raced with scenarios... How could I get everyone out of this mess? Maybe I should have let Bleeker drive us around for a few hours to buy some time.

"Pit stop." I adjusted a torn strip of my sparkly dress.

Bleeker turned down the music's volume. "Pit stop?" He frowned.

"I have to go." I waited for the light bulb to blink on in his eyes. "To the bathroom."

"Mia." He shook his head. "For heaven's sake. We've been getting along so well, but—"

"I can't help it. I haven't gone in hours. I've had a large soda. I can't concentrate on portal finding if I have to pee—"

He held up his hand to stop me. "Bathroom break. We'll stop." He pulled over and stopped. "Here?"

"You're kidding, right?" I didn't have to fake horrified. I couldn't step out into the ditch and pee.

"Then we'll have to go back to the lab. Nothing will be open for your emergency stop." He shifted back into drive and made a wide U-turn in the middle of the highway.

I hoped that Regulus was gone. Actually needing to go to the bathroom as well wanting to stall for time, I hadn't thought we'd turn around and go back to the building we'd left.

As we approached the building I now knew was a lab, I smelled something foreign in the night air. A fiery light glowed in back of the lab, and smoke billowed, shadowing the stream of light cast by the streetlamp.

My mouth dropped open. Bleeker stopped the vehicle on the side of the road before we reached the parking lot. I heard sirens coming in our direction.

"What did you do?" Bleeker growled at me through gritted teeth.

Confused, I turned to look at him, and he slapped me on my right jaw. My head snapped back and bobbled for a minute. The stinging blow burned into my face, and I sat slack-jawed. I was speechless. Slapping seemed so much more personal than being threatened with a gun or knife.

"Oh man, you don't hit her." Tiny's deep voice boomed from the back.

Out of the corner of my eye, I could see Tiny in the backseat being physically restrained with a gun pointed at him. Red-faced, he looked ready to explode.

"I'm OK," I managed to say to Tiny. "I didn't do anything. The fire..." It dawned on me that Regulus had done this. "Something must have happened in your lab after we left. We were with you the entire time."

Dr. Bleeker was staring at the building as the fire burned brighter. A loud pop sounded from somewhere inside, and the flames reached higher. Bleeker's nostrils flared, and his normally pleasant face twisted into a grimace.

I heard a buzz, and Bleeker took a cell phone from his jacket pocket.

"Yes. I know." Pause. "Maybe not." Another pause. "Leave it. The fire department won't find anything... As soon as I send these kids through." Bleeker snapped his phone shut.

My head started to pound, and I rubbed my temples and forehead. I could feel the hot skin swelling on my cheek where Bleeker had hit me. I saw him watching me, and I put my hands in my lap.

"I apologize. I shouldn't have let my emotions get the best of me. Stress. You know how it is." His voice was honey-coated.

I nodded like I understood. The ringing in my ears hadn't subsided yet.

"Calm down, big man," Bleeker said to Tiny.

A police car screeched to a halt, blocking off the

highway in front of us. I could see a fire truck already in the parking lot ahead. I jumped as another loud explosion ricocheted metal into the air. Some fell in front of the Hummer. Debris flew, and firemen rushed out with hoses to spray the flaming mass nearest our vehicle.

I twisted my head to make sure Austin's Jeep was still behind us. A fireman came to the window and motioned for Bleeker to roll it down. He obeyed, and smoke began to roll inside. My eyes burned.

"Holy smokes," Bleeker said to the person in his window. "We're passing through. Can we go by?"

"There is an officer ahead who is blocking traffic into the area near the fire. He'll stop you," the voice said. Then the man bent and put his head in the window, forcing Bleeker to roll it down all the way.

Cade from our disastrous trip to Goliath stared at me. He grinned.

I avoided looking at him. When I glanced over, his brows had knitted together in a confused upside-down V. He was looking from Bleeker to me, then to Tiny and the two guards in the backseat.

"My family and I are driving through looking for a gas station." Bleeker pressed the button to open the window fully. "My daughter, Cindy, needs to find a restroom. I hope this doesn't take long."

"Wait right here." Cade strode to the police car.

Bleeker cursed under his breath. I shrank back against the seat, hoping he wouldn't slap me again. I'd be ready this time to dodge a blow.

The Hummer lurched from a standstill to flying in seconds. I grabbed the console as Bleeker drove into the ditch and past Cade, the police car, the fire, and town. I turned to see Tiny looking as white as a sheet, and the Jeep headlights following on our tail.

"You're going to get us killed," I screamed.

"Sit back!" He flung out his arm to pin me against the seat. "And think portal thoughts."

Blue lights flashed in the rearview mirror. The sound of the officer's siren filled me with relief and dread. It was good to know that I might have some help in getting us out of this. It was bad because I didn't know how I would explain this one to my father.

Bumping and jerking, we'd completely left the road. I peered around to see that a grinning Tiny had knocked out one of the guards and had the other in a headlock. I tried to see where the weapons were in the backseat.

We were driving off-road through a field of rice when Bleeker hit the brakes. My hands slammed into the front windshield. Pain stabbed through my wrists.

He pulled a gun from his jacket and pointed it at Tiny. "Change of plan," Bleeker said. "My lab is destroyed. My presence here is known. This portal will be of no use to me. I need another."

"I'll find another one. Let Tiny and my friends go," I said. "You only need me."

"OK, out!" he barked at Tiny, pointing at the door.

I looked around the rice field. The sun was beginning to rise, and the Hummer was alone in the field.

"You're not going to shoot him when he gets out, are you?" I said.

Bleeker's mouth twitched at one corner. "That

would be silly, Mia. We're friends, you and I. You have to trust me if we are going to work together in the future. Now, get out. Mia stays and everyone else gets out."

Tiny looked as confused as I felt. He loosened his headlock on the guard who was still conscious. The other one had slumped to the door like he was taking a nap.

"They are useless if they can't be counted on to stop an unarmed boy like you." Tiny's eyebrows shot up.

"Go, Tiny. Before he changes his mind. I'll be fine," I said calmly.

Tiny grimaced and nodded. He really didn't have much choice with a gun pointed at him anyway. He opened the door and dragged the guy pinned under his arm out of the Hummer. Then he punched him. Hard. The guard's knees buckled, and he was out.

"The other one too," Bleeker said as he motioned with the gun toward the far door.

Tiny walked around the Hummer to open the door and let the man fall the ground. Tiny had no sooner closed the Hummer door when Bleeker accelerated again, driving toward the end of the field.

The bright, beautiful sun rose, slowly filling the vehicle with light. I leaned my head back against the seat and closed my eyes. My life was over. Bleeker was kidnapping me, and I'd be lucky to stay alive long enough to find the next portal for him. I was glad that Tiny had escaped. Fighting back tears, I thought of Em, Austin, and Regulus. I didn't know where they were, but I hoped they'd make it.

I opened my eyes to see that we had left the field.

The Hummer easily crawled up a ditch to enter a road. It was early morning and deserted.

The snarl of an engine caught my attention, and I glanced back to see a motorcycle behind us. I straightened up and looked in the passenger-side rearview mirror, then at the speedometer. We were doing about fifty-five in the Hummer.

The motorcycle weaved out as if to pass us, and I recognized both bike and driver. Regulus had on a helmet, dark sunglasses, and those familiar black cargo pants he loved because of all the pockets. My stomach dropped before a thrill of excitement, relief, and fear raced through my body.

Bleeker looked in the rearview mirror. "Shit." He pointed at me. "You are causing me heartburn. This can be easy or it can be hard. Call the motorcycle boyfriend off." He held up the gun. "Before I put a bullet in his head."

How had he known about Regulus? Did everyone have a big spy camera pointed at me? "He's not my boyfriend," I said without thinking. "Not anymore. You know you people…all of you…think you can pull me this way and that to make me do things you want me to do without asking my opinion—"

"Shut the hell up," he bellowed. "You're distracting me." He slammed his foot onto the accelerator. The Hummer sped and swerved from one side of the road to the other, as though he was flooring it.

"The road!" I screamed and looked ahead while grabbing onto the dash with one hand and my door handle with the other. The Hummer hugged the curve, and I took a deep shuddering breath. One minute we were on the road, the next we were bouncing across an uneven field.

My tongue was bleeding from having bitten it at some point. I was tossed around so hard I couldn't turn to see if Regulus was still behind us. The sunlight filtered through the windshield brightly, and I couldn't see.

Bleeker reached down, away from the steering wheel.

"What are you doing?" I asked, blurting each word out like a single sentence as my head bounced up and down.

Then I saw the gun in the floor.

Bleeker had dropped his gun.

I unbuckled my seatbelt, ducked, and lunged for it, desperate to get it first. It was lodged at the edge of the floorboard near Bleeker's seat. He used one hand to feel for the gun and the other to grab my head, trying to stop me.

That meant that he wasn't steering the speeding Hummer.

I felt along the floorboard. It was sliding around, and I had only luck and a few moments to find it.

My head slammed into plastic and body. Everything tilted.

The Hummer had collided with something.

And then my world went black.

* * *

"You coming with her?" A deep voice yelled over the whirring noise of the wind.

"Yes," a familiar male voice answered.

"Jump in. We'll take care of the motorcycle."

"She is going to live?"

"We'll keep her going until we can get her to the hospital. The 'copter's fast. We'll be there in no time."

"I need to make sure she does not die."

"No problem. We patch 'em up worse than this."

I reached out a hand. "Regulus?" I was chilled, my teeth clicking together rapidly.

"Yes?"

"You missed the dance," I whispered. "You missed it all."

A warm hand closed around mine. I let out a deep sigh of relief.

"Yes. I...I think I've missed something."

I smiled even though it hurt. Then I drifted to the sounds of wind pulsing around my head.

Chapter Seventeen

Austin

"You have a second to decide if I know how to use this thing or not." Em pointed the silver box at the woman in the back seat of the Jeep.

Austin couldn't stop staring at the woman in his rearview mirror. She looked so much like Mia. How could anyone doubt she was Mia's mother? The truck driver blasted his horn, and Austin jerked his gaze back to the road in time to stay in his lane. He glanced at Em.

A high-pitched whine shrilled from the box. The woman fell over like a cut tree.

"Wow." Em's voice came out in a deep exhale. "That worked better than I thought."

Austin craned his head to see. "Did you kill her?" he asked while pulling over. "You didn't kill her, right? For crying out loud, tell me she's not dead." He parked, then took several deep breaths and reached back to snare the handgun that had fallen on the seat. Gingerly, he reached across to place his fingers on the woman's neck.

"Well?" Em fidgeted. "Alive?"

"Yeah. She's got a pulse. How long do you think she'll be out?" Hearing a chime, Austin reached inside his jacket for his phone. He read the text to Em. "Get help. Mia needs medical." He dropped his face into his hands and rested his forehead on the steering wheel.

"No. You get yourself together right now," Em said. "I'm calling nine-one-one."

"Wait, "Austin said, lifting his head. "Just one second. I'm going to log in to *Quest.*"

"Are you insane?" Em's eyes were huge. She blinked hard.

"Pete," he said. Austin's thumbs were a flurry of motion. "You can call 911, but I'm letting Pete know what's gone down here."

"Deal." Em voice wavered. "How do I tell them where she is?"

"Stop, Em. Pete answered me. He said he's got it. He said that med-flight is on its way."

"How—"

"Dude's got connections." Austin set the phone on the dash, and then rubbed his face.

"What do we do with her?" Em tilted a head to the back. "Take her back to Officer Sanchez?"

Austin placed both hands behind his head and leaned back. "And say what? This lady held us at gunpoint 'cause she works for an evil professor who kidnapped Mia since she can spot a thing called a portal, but Mia's now hurt and her brother who has been missing…" He stopped when he saw Em shaking her head slowly back and forth.

"How about another choice?"

"I say we dump her here." Austin peered out at the desolate highway. Smiling, he added, "It's what Mia would want. Just leave her like she's unwanted baggage."

"I can live with that." Em opened her door. "I'll carry her feet if you'll get the heavy end."

"Done. Let's hurry. I've also had a text from Tiny. He sent me his GPS coordinates. He's on foot."

"And Mia?" Em hesitated with her hand still on the door, ready to get out.

"Pete says he'll let me know where they're taking her." Austin closed his eyes and took a deep breath. He felt a hand on his arm.

"She'll be OK." Em paused, then said, "We'll be there. Together."

He nodded. "Let's get Mommy Dearest out of the back and into the ditch."

Chapter Eighteen

Starting Over

Opening my eyes felt like ripping a Band-Aid off a bloody wound. The stinging, sticky sensation alarmed me because I couldn't move my hand to wipe my eyes. I wrinkled my nose. It felt dry and sore.

I was in a hospital room. That much I knew. Em lay asleep in a chair beside me, still wearing her pretty formal. My dad was in the other chair.

I wondered if this meant I'd be grounded for the remainder of my senior year. Maybe even through college.

"Hey," I said.

My dad's eyes flew open and leaned forward. "Hello, Sleeping Beauty."

One corner of my mouth was all I could manage to move. "Water?"

"One minute, sweetie." He rose and slipped out of the room.

"You're awake." Em's eyes shimmered with tears.

"How did—" I began.

"Shh. I'll tell you everything later. Rest," she said.

"Regulus?"

"He's fine. Austin and Tiny are fine. We're OK. Listen, your dad will be back in a second. This is what you need to know right now. You and Regulus had a motorcycle wreck. Here in town. We did not leave Whispering Woods."

"But—"

"That's the story."

Dad walked back in with a Styrofoam cup and bent the straw to my mouth. "Take a sip. You can have as much as you want."

I nodded. Or I thought I nodded. The act of moving my head was exhausting. The cold water felt wonderful in my throat. I smiled and closed my eyes again.

*   *   *

"Time for some more meds."

I pushed the hand away, but it wouldn't leave. I cracked one eye open. A young woman in pink scrubs stood beside my bed. She put the paper cup down on the overbed table. "Breakfast will be here soon."

Dad sat up in his chair and rubbed his eyes with one hand while stifling a yawn with the other. "Sleep OK?"

"Mm." I lifted my head. Em was gone.

The nurse shook pills from the cup into my hand. "Can you take them yourself, or do you need my help?"

I lifted my arm to reach my mouth in answer. Every movement seemed like it was slow motion. I got the pills into my mouth and looked at the nurse for directions. Smiling, she held a straw to my lips.

"Wash those down and we'll get you something to eat," she said.

Dad looked tired. He'd obviously slept in his clothes in the hospital chair. But he winked at me and smiled.

"When's the doctor going to do rounds?" he asked the nurse.

She looked at her watch. "In half an hour or so."

An orderly entered with a full tray. "Here's breakfast."

My nurse set up the bed tray over my waist and bent to push a button on the bed, lifting my upper body into a seated position. "I'm Ally, your day nurse. I'll be checking on you throughout the day. Call me if you need anything." She opened the milk carton and poured the contents into a plastic mug.

Dad and I watched her leave. I turned to him. "She was cute," I said slowly with my tongue seeming too big for my mouth.

He shook his head and laughed. "She's almost your age. Quit matchmaking."

"Mature. Seemed mature." I managed to say the words, but talking was like struggling through deep snow. I stared at the breakfast tray in front of me. "Want some?"

He shook his head.

"Have to eat. You." I knew I sounded crazy.

"If I run down to the cafeteria, do you promise me you'll try to eat some of yours?"

"Yeah, yeah. Go." I attempted to wave my right hand. My left hand was bandaged.

"I'll stay," he said.

"No." I picked up a triangle of toast. "See? Eating."

He looked relieved. "Back in fifteen or twenty minutes. I need about a pot of coffee." He tossed one last glance over his shoulder as he headed for the door.

I set down the toast and gratefully drank the milk straight from the carton. There was no way I was eating the lump of yellow scrambled eggs. I settled my head back against the pillows and closed my eyes.

"How's breakfast?"

I didn't open my eyes. The voice came at me with a tidal wave of emotion and want and memory.

I had to be dreaming.

"You can't be asleep that fast. I'm sure you were wrestling with the milk carton."

I opened my eyes but still believed I was dreaming. The familiar young man in front of me wore blue scrubs and a stethoscope around his neck. He scooted a chair up to the edge of the bed.

"Pete?" My throat was tight, and I could barely get the word out. Confused, I shook my head.

"Yeah. You dress up like this and you have free rein of this place."

I stared. "You're back? Am I awake?"

"Just making sure that my baby sis is OK," he said. "I only have a couple of minutes." He took my left hand and examined the bandage. "Hurt much?"

I ignored the question. "Where? Why?"

"I chose not to work for the IIA. They don't like to be turned down. I never thought they'd force you to join them."

"Bleeker?"

"What? No, no." He shook his head. "I'm US military. Special unit. Very special."

"Can you stay a little while?" I felt like I was five years old again.

"No. Can't, Mia." He held my bandaged hand. "Gotta make this quick. Cafeteria's got a long line, but Dad will be back soon."

"Why did you come then?"

"I'm watching out for you. You should know you're not alone."

"I feel alone," I said, remembering that Regulus didn't even remember me.

"I know you're involved with Regulus. I need to warn you."

"Not anymore."

"Did you two break up? When I sent the helicopter, he insisted on riding with you."

"You sent the helicopter?" I wasn't even sure what had happened, so that made no sense to me.

"Yeah. Regulus called his partner for help. Then Austin messaged me through *Quest*."

I screwed up my face in confusion.

"On his phone, Mia."

I nodded. "About Regulus. I'm a stranger to him, Pete. I don't know why he wanted to come with me." I blinked hard and took a deep breath.

"Stranger?"

"He doesn't even remember me." I choked out the words. "They did something to him."

"Oh," Pete said. He leaned forward and kissed my cheek. "Listen carefully. It's not his fault. When they did it to Mom, it wasn't her fault."

"What?" I totally lost control now, and tears started to stream down my face.

"Mia, you have to be brave and stop crying. Dad is going to come back and wonder what happened in the last few minutes." He looked at the door. An unfamiliar nurse appeared in the doorway.

"He's coming back," she told Pete.

"I love you, sis. Don't think you're alone. And be careful." He jumped to his feet and backed away to the door.

"Pete?"

"What?"

"Take care of yourself. I'll be fine." I tried to smile and knew it was lame.

He put two fingers to his forehead in a salute. "Yes, ma'am." He turned and disappeared through the doorway.

"Mia?"

"Huh?" My dad's voice surprised me and I looked up while holding my breath.

"Did I miss the doctor?"

"No, why?"

"I thought I saw a man leaving this room." Dad walked over to the chair he'd slept in last night. Pete had moved it to the side of my bed. "Was somebody here?"

"Somebody from the hospital checking on me."

He came over and wiped a thumb across my

cheek. "Have you been crying, sweetie? Are you in pain?"

"You'd cry too if you had to eat this," I said and pushed the tray away.

He laughed.

"I'm fine. Only emotional," I said.

My dad produced a white paper take-out bag. "Don't tell. I snuck this from the cafeteria." He offered a biscuit on a napkin to me. "Sausage and cheese," he said.

I took it from him and grinned. "Thanks for the contraband."

He winked. "I have to get your strength up so we can get you out of this place." He went to the door. "Eat up. I'll watch out for the food police."

* * *

The next day, my doctor released me, and I went home. Dad grounded me for another month. I thought it would be longer, but he said that I'd learned my lesson. I really think he was tired of me being grounded and moping around the house.

There was also the fact that I'd told him that Regulus and I had broken up. I could tell Dad felt sorry for me. I didn't mind being grounded. I went to school, did homework, and talked to Em on the phone.

Em told me how she and Austin had found the stunner that Arizona had handed me the night we'd gone to Goliath. It was still in the Jeep. I'm such a great agent that I'd left my weapon in the vehicle when I ran to the building. Em had managed to use it on Nancy by remembering my description of how the weapon worked. I had laughed until I cried.

They'd left her unconscious on the side of the road when Tiny had called, finding him using his GPS coordinates. Finding me had been harder. The Hummer had hit an irrigation pump in the field and rolled. I'd been thrown clear, but injured. Regulus had called Arizona, who'd called Austin for help. Because of Regulus's chip, Arizona had known exactly where we were.

Em and Austin dropped by one day to bring me what they called a care package of candy and CDs they'd bought. I told them about talking with Pete at the hospital. They listened to the story in silence and didn't respond or seem surprised when I told them the part where Pete had mentioned Nancy.

Thanksgiving came and went. I decided to redecorate my room. Em came over to help me take down posters and miscellaneous things. It was time for a new era in my life, which meant getting rid of Pete's hand-me-down decorations. We worked side by side while listening to music until lunchtime. I made peanut butter and jelly sandwiches and brought those upstairs on a tray.

After taking down all the stuff, my room appeared colorless and unloved. We sat on my bed and ate the sandwiches while watching a reality show on my tiny bedroom TV. I stared at the screen but couldn't remember anything about the teenagers being filmed or the constant drama on the screen.

"Snap out of it, Mia."

"What do you mean?" I looked at Em blankly.

"It will get better. But it won't this way."

"I'm fine." I tore off a bread crust and dropped it on my plate.

"Arizona called me yesterday. Regulus wants to see you," she said. "He wants to talk."

I was shocked and nervous at the same time. All the air left my body, and I couldn't drag more in. "Why?"

Em shrugged. "Hey, he didn't tell me anything. I mean, I did ask if he suddenly got his memory back," she said sarcastically.

"He didn't do it to himself, Em. The IIA did it and you know that."

She nodded. "I know."

"He probably wants to make sure that I'll still be a portal finder for them."

She looked at her watch. "He'll be here in five minutes."

My mouth dropped open. "No, he can't. I can't see him today."

"Avoiding him isn't going to work. You said yourself that it isn't his fault."

The doorbell rang. I shot Em a dirty look.

"Thanks for the heads up. You are such a traitor." I walked to the door. "Aren't you coming?"

"No. I'm watching this show," she said as she waved her half-eaten sandwich at the television.

I thudded down each step, feeling as though my feet weighed twenty pounds each. Dad was gone for the day, and Biscuit barked excitedly while running back and forth at the doorway. As soon as I opened the door, Biscuit ran outside and circled Regulus, who bent to rub Biscuit's head and ears.

"Hello," he said from his bent position.

I sucked air and tried to breathe. Air in, air out.

His dark blue eyes weren't hostile, but they weren't friendly either. He seemed...wary. I bet he was as nervous as I was. Did he think I was mad?

"Hi," I said and stepped out onto the porch. I crossed my arms over my chest. "Em said you needed to talk to me about something?"

He straightened, but shifted from one foot to the other. He gestured at the porch swing. "Can we sit down?"

I stared at it and couldn't stand the thought of sitting that close to him. I'd done that so many times. All those times, we'd sat in the middle and he'd have his arm slung over my shoulders.

"I'm fine." A wood railing ran the length of the porch. I perched on it.

"I know that you are wondering why I am here." He looked around.

"Yeah." I waited.

"I need to ask you some questions."

"Shoot."

His eyebrows jerked up.

"Ask away," I said. I forced myself to look at the collar of his down jacket instead of into his eyes.

"Why did you follow me to Goliath?"

I shrugged. "You needed backup. You weren't going to ask for it."

He nodded. "The IIA is important to you."

"No, not really." I hesitated. "I do want to stop Bleeker, and I'm sorry he got away. That's the only agenda I have."

"Oh," he said. "Then you did it to stop Bleeker." His eyes looked as though they were...searching.

What did he want from me?

"I did it to make sure you didn't get yourself killed," I said.

"And that would matter to you?"

"Yes, it would matter." I looked away again. My throat was tightening. "But I understand that you don't remember us...me. It's cool. Don't worry about it."

He shoved his hands into his pockets and turned away. "Do you know what déjà vu is?" he asked quietly, voice so soft I almost didn't hear him.

"Of course, I do. Why?"

"Something will happen... I'll be in class and a girl will toss her hair and I'll catch a scent of her shampoo. And in my mind I will see you. In that moment, I will think of your hair and the smell. I can feel the texture. I can see the exact color. I think it is something that has already happened. I would say that it is a...déjà vu moment for me."

I nodded because I didn't know what to say. His confession was making me sadder than ever. I could see that he'd come trying to figure things out.

"I'm sorry. I don't know how the cleanse works. Maybe the déjà vu thing will go away over time. I don't know what to tell you."

He stared at me, gaze searching my face, my hair, and sliding down my body. What was he trying to answer?

"What if I told you that I don't want it to go away." He came closer.

I edged away, scooting along the porch rail. My

chest and throat were tightening. I thought of the IIA and the cleansing. I thought of Pete and what he'd said about our mother.

"We can be friends. It's all good. I'm still your portal finder." I wanted to say anything to stop the conversation. I longed for him to turn and leave so I could escape to my room.

"Friends." He nodded. "I will see you soon, then...friend."

"Sure. Be safe on that thing." I eyed the motorcycle.

I heard him murmur something under his breath.

"What did you say?"

"For I ne'er saw true beauty till this night." He paused. "It's a line from my lit class. William Shakespeare. I cannot get the one line out of my head. I have been studying for finals too much." He laughed softly.

I watched him leave and take my heart with him. Regulus had once said he'd carry me in his heart always. Maybe it was true.

The End